FROM THAT MOMENT

A Promise Me Novel

CARRIE ANN RYAN

FROM THAT MOMENT

A PROMISE ME NOVEL

By
Carrie Ann Ryan

FROM THAT MOMENT
A Promise Me Novel
By: Carrie Ann Ryan
© 2020 Carrie Ann Ryan
ISBN: 978-1-947007-90-1
Cover Art by Sweet N Spicy Designs
Photograph by Wander Photography

Praise for Carrie Ann Ryan

"Count on Carrie Ann Ryan for emotional, sexy, character driven stories that capture your heart!" – Carly Phillips, NY Times bestselling author

"Carrie Ann Ryan's romances are my newest addiction! The emotion in her books captures me from the very beginning. The hope and healing hold me close until the end. These love stories will simply sweep you away." ~ NYT Bestselling Author Deveny Perry

"Carrie Ann Ryan writes the perfect balance of sweet and heat ensuring every story feeds the soul." - Audrey Carlan, #1 New York Times Bestselling Author

"Carrie Ann Ryan never fails to draw readers in with passion, raw sensuality, and characters that pop off the page. Any book by Carrie Ann is an absolute treat." – New York Times Bestselling Author J. Kenner

"Carrie Ann Ryan knows how to pull your heartstrings and make your pulse pound! Her wonderful Redwood Pack series will draw you in and keep you reading long into the night. I can't wait to see what comes next with the new generation, the Talons. Keep them coming, Carrie Ann!" –Lara Adrian, New York Times bestselling author of CRAVE THE NIGHT

To our Essential Workers
Thank you.
Thank you.

Acknowledgments

I wanted to write a story about officemates who hated each other and somehow it turned into something far more. Thank you Nana Malone for helping me figure out exactly what that meant!

Thank you Chelle for wrangling my words and my mind. I know this one wasn't easy for many reasons, but it's so much shinier because of you.

Thank you Jaycee for this cover. This might be my favorite cover of yours. Ever.

And thank you to Wander for this image! They are the perfect Prior and Paris!!

And as always, thank you dear readers for going on this journey with me. I hope you love the Brady Brothers and the PROMISE ME series!

Happy reading, everyone!
~Carrie Ann

From that Moment

New York Times and USA Today bestselling author Carrie Ann Ryan continues her sexy new contemporary stand-alone series with an enemies-to-lovers office romance.

Paris Trissel is in a dating rut. Despite the pact she made with her friends to find someone to share her life with, she's throwing in the towel after only a few blind dates. Add in the fact that the new hire at the job she used to love happens to be the Brady brother she can't stand, and Paris is having a terrible year.

Prior Brady's life seems pretty perfect from the outside. He has a wonderful, caring girlfriend, a family he's never been closer to, and a new job he can't wait to sink his teeth and talents into. Too bad the woman he has to work with for hours a day hates him on sight.

Once the two are forced to find the balance between chemistry and temptation, however, they'll realize they're stronger together than apart. Except when Paris's past comes back with a vengeance, bringing terror, pain, and horror with it, both she and Prior will have to lean on each other.

In more ways than one.

Chapter 1

Prior

"I THINK YOU'RE GOING TO LIKE IT HERE, THOUGH I still don't know why you only want to stay for six months. I don't know, once you meet everybody, you might want to stay for a bit longer. There are some perks." Benji elbowed me in the ribs, though it wasn't hard enough to hurt, and then he winked. "If you know what I mean."

I looked at the other man and kept a pleasant smile on my face. I hoped to hell I had no idea what he meant. Because if this was the start of my new job, then it was going to be a long fucking six months.

I was going to take this job today and be here for the next half a year. The branch wanted me to plug up a hole that people kept revolving through over the past year or so.

I was a software engineer and was damn good at my job. Working on a project usually took longer than six months. However, turnover on this one seemed greater than normal.

I'd always wanted to work for this department of the company, even in a temporary position. When my current branch offered to loan me out, I greedily accepted.

I loved my current job, but I adored the fact that I could work with another team for a little while. It wasn't that unheard of when both branches were owned by the same conglomerate. The fact that I got bored easily, even with jobs I loved, meant that this was a perfect break for me. It wasn't the first time I had done it, but it was the first time I'd felt so uneasy about the guy talking to me.

Benji had been working at this particular branch for the past six years and had moved up in the ranks quickly. I had seen his work and appreciated what it did for the company. I hadn't spoken to him in person before, though. Now, I understood why that had probably been a good thing for both of us.

"So is my office this way?" I asked, changing the subject. I didn't want to wonder what Benji was talking about for long. Not if I wanted to keep this job.

"Oh, yes. You're right next door to your software quality engineer."

"That'll be helpful, considering she's going to check all of my work for the next six months."

Benji rolled his eyes. "She'll probably give you a hard time about it, too. She loves telling us everything we do wrong."

I frowned, grateful that no one was around to overhear.

"That's sort of her job, isn't it?" I asked. "I mean, I develop it, and she tests it. There's always going to be kinks in the system that we need to figure out."

"I think she enjoys telling men that they're wrong. If you know what I mean."

I hated that phrase.

I held back a sigh and resisted the urge to pinch the bridge of my nose. Oh, good. It was going to be one of *those* places. I couldn't wait.

"So, here's your office," Benji said, moving into a nicely sized room with a desk, a couple of tables against the walls, and a bright window.

I was going to love that view and natural light.

At my current place, I shared an office with someone because the rooms were about twice the size of these. And my office mate hated light. Seriously, I was pretty sure he was a vampire. That meant my beautiful window always had its blinds closed. No matter what I did, I resolved myself to the fact that I would never be able to see the outside world again from my office.

At least that's how it felt. That's why I did my best to work from home most days.

Considering my job, I was able to do that. I kind of liked this office so far, though. Maybe I would work onsite more often. I'd have to see how things worked. For instance, if Benji continued on his path of freaking me out, maybe I'd telecommute. I guess it all depended on my software quality engineer.

For all I knew, they did have it out for every developer out there and enjoyed telling us what was wrong.

What I didn't like was the fact that the man sounded fucking sexist when he said it. I would like to see and form my own opinions.

"Looks great," I said and turned to Benji. "Thanks. Seriously. I'll be back tomorrow to start for real, but I'm thankful that you showed me around today."

"I'm glad you're going to be here. Even though it's only six months, maybe you'll like it. We always like new blood. It gets kind of annoying after a while when everyone just leaves because they're afraid of the Shark."

"Excuse me?" I asked, confused and a little weary.

"Yes, Benji. Excuse me?" a very familiar voice said

from behind us. I turned and could have cursed under my breath.

Paris. Of course, it was Paris.

The one person in the area that I knew, who legit acted as if she hated me, though I had no idea why.

Paris, the best friend of the woman who was marrying my brother.

Oh, yes, *that* Paris.

"Hey, didn't see you there," Benji said, his hand on his tie, running his fingers down the length as if he hadn't just been bad-mouthing someone.

And I *knew* it had to have been about Paris. It had to be given the way the two were acting.

"No, you wouldn't with your back to me. If you're going to talk crap about me and call me names like you love to do, I would make sure that the door isn't open, and you're not saying it for everybody to hear." Paris crossed her arms over her chest and glared at me. "*You.* You're the new software engineer? Of course, you are. Because why not have more of the boys' club here?"

My brows went up to my hairline, and I held up my hands. "Hey, what the hell?"

"Don't *what the hell* me. If I ever hear you saying the word *Shark* around here, I will make sure you don't last another day. I mean, it's not like you will anyway. Right? No one else has."

"Wait. You guys know each other?" Benji asked, his gaze darting between us.

"We're friends," I said.

"Uh, no, we aren't."

I looked at Paris and raised a single brow this time. "We've broken bread together. We hang out because your friend is marrying my brother. I would assume we're friends."

"And you would assume wrong. We are forced into each other's proximity because of people we care about. That doesn't make us friends."

"Okay, then," I said softly. "That's going to make the upcoming wedding and everything else fucking hard, isn't it?"

"Don't curse. This is work."

"You're right. I'm sorry about that. Also, I wasn't the one who called you that name." I turned to Benji. "And Benji isn't going to be saying it again, will you?"

Benji held up both hands. "No, I promise. I'll be good."

"Whatever," Paris said. "I guess you're starting tomorrow? Good. Just know you better work hard because I don't take lackluster work from anyone. I'm good at my job. If you have a problem with that, let me know now so I can deal with it because I'm going to be the one telling you when you do things wrong. If you have a problem hearing that from me, get over it now."

Benji slid out of the door past Paris, leaving the two of us alone in the office.

I shook my head, wondering what the fuck was going on.

"Can you close the door for a second?"

"Uh, no. Why the hell would I do that?"

"Language," I said, teasing at first. When her eyes narrowed, I lifted my chin, steadying my gaze. "Let's talk, okay? I'm as surprised as you. I didn't know you worked here. Honestly. Let's get everything out in the open. However, considering that Benji—and God knows who else—probably has his ears pressed against his door trying to listen in, let's get some privacy."

Paris narrowed her eyes, then took a few steps into my office, closing the door behind her.

"Fine. I'll give you two minutes." She did a show of looking at her watch, and I barely resisted the urge to chuckle.

"Okay, since I'm on a timer, what's wrong?"

Paris just glared at me. "I don't know, maybe this hostile work environment."

"You're the one sniping at me when we didn't even get to fully introduce ourselves. I don't even fucking know your last name."

Color tinged her cheeks, but she didn't back down.

"Trissel. Paris Trissel. And I know you're one of the Brady brothers. Though not the fun bunch, are you?"

"Ha-ha. I've never once heard a *Brady Bunch* joke in my life. Gasp. You were the first person to ever make one. Ever."

"Prior."

"No. Let's get this out. I don't know why you don't like me. Maybe you don't like anyone. That's your prerogative. We're going to be working together for the next six months, and yes, you're going to be checking my work. Thank God. I'm going to make some mistakes. Hopefully, not ones that break the whole damn system, but I'm going to make mistakes. I'm going to need help getting the bugs out. And that's your job."

"And you don't mind the fact that I'm going to be the one scrutinizing your work?"

"Paris. You're good at what you do."

"And how do you know that?"

"Because Hazel and the other girls constantly say that you're brilliant and tell me about what you do. I just didn't think you worked *here*. I never asked."

She blinked at me. "The girls said that?"

"Of course. You are all smart, talented women." I purposely didn't say *beautiful* because we were at work, but Paris was fucking hot.

Long, dark hair and a slender body with curves in all the right places. I had taken note before, of course, and I was kicking myself that I had noticed in the way I had.

Today, she even wore glasses, big square ones that were in fashion these days, and that only made her look hotter.

In fact, she had worn these glasses before, and I'd had a fantasy of her bent over my desk as I...okay, enough of that.

We were working together now, and I had Allison, my girlfriend. So not the images I should have in my mind.

"I need your help here, Paris."

"So you say. But you were in here with Benji when he was talking how he usually does." She blew her bangs from her face, kind of fogging up her glasses a bit as she did, and I held back a smile.

She was so damn cute. I shouldn't be thinking that at all. Only, it was the friend part of my brain that did so. And I had to keep that thought from my mind because it would be rude as fuck to say something like that about a coworker. I needed to change the way I thought about Paris.

I could do it. At least for six months. Right?

"I thought that Benji was a jerk, and I was going to call him out on it, but then you walked in.?

"So you say," she said. And once again, I resisted the urge to roll my eyes.

"It's the truth, Paris. You don't have to believe me, but hopefully, you'll see it eventually. I'm not the asshole you think I am." I paused. "I know...*language.*"

She turned away from me, letting out a long breath. "They call me the Shark. You heard that?"

"I did. I thought it was a good thing in our line of work. I don't think it is from your tone or his."

"They call me Shark because I smell blood in the water when it comes to mistakes, and they like making fun of my period."

"Excuse me?" I asked, my hands fisting at my sides. "You've got to be fucking kidding me."

"Oh, they haven't said it out loud to me, but I heard one of the guys whispering about it once. So, I'm going to assume that's what he meant."

"Fucking assholes. Why do you put up with it?"

"You're serious? I put up with it because I love what I do, I make damn good money, it has a fantastic health insurance plan, and...as I said, *I'm damn good at my job.* I'd have to deal with this no matter where I went. So, they can all be leery of me and just watch me do my best work, or I can whine about it to the boss constantly and never get anywhere."

"Jesus," I grumbled. "You don't have to worry about that from me. I'm not one of those guys."

"I guess we'll have to see, won't we?" she asked, lifting her chin. "Because you're only here for six months. I've been here for a long damn time. This is where I want to stay. So don't fuck this up for me. And yes, language. See what you made me do? I've become Paris in the streets, rather than Paris at work."

The fact that my mind went to Paris and the *sheets* was something I'd have to deal with.

"Remember, we work together. You aren't my boss, and I'm not yours. So, don't even think about trying to order me around."

Now I was getting pissed off. "I wasn't thinking that. Did you not hear me when I said that I like quality assurance? I mean, hell, I told you I'm going to make mistakes. I need someone to help me clean them up. If you're going to be a jerk about it, then I *might* get angry."

"Well, I guess we'll have to see, won't we?"

"Are you ever going to tell me why you hate me so much?"

"I just said—"

I cut her off. "No, not right now. From before. You've always grumbled about me and around me. At every dinner or event that we do as a group, you always growl at me. It's the same way Myra growls at Nate, and Dakota practically hides from Macon. I don't know what's going on with all of you guys, but I'm sick of it. Unless you stop being friends with Hazel, we'll be stuck in the vicinity of each other for a long damn time. And now that I'm working here for the next six months? We're going to be working closely. So, stop hating me and start working with me."

"I don't hate you. I just don't like you."

This time, I laughed. "You don't even know me."

"No, I don't, but you're like all the guys here. And I've had to fight to get where I am. And I'm tired of it. I like my job, and people like Benji make it harder and harder for me to continue liking it. Maybe I'm a bitch, but people can fuck right off."

"You're not a bitch," I grumbled. I didn't even like saying the word.

"Far from it. You just like things done right. As you should. You may hate me on sight, but I'm not going to use that word."

"Whatever." And then she froze, cursing herself.

"Great, I've been in here longer than two minutes, and now everyone's going to think I'm fucking the new employee."

"If I hear anything, I'll put those rumors to rest. Because no matter where I work, I don't take kindly to assholes putting women down. Putting *anyone* down for that matter."

"You say that, and yet they're going to be high-fiving you while calling me a whore."

I counted to ten so I wouldn't say something I'd regret later. "Why do you love this place so much if that's how you automatically think?"

"Because it hasn't happened here yet. It happened at the last place I worked. I'm used to it. I'm a woman in a man's world. It's what happens. However, I'm done playing nice about it."

Her phone buzzed, and she looked down at it as if she weren't even thinking and then paled.

"What is it?"

"Nothing. Just stupid pact stuff."

That made me smile. I knew about the pact. The four women—Hazel, Paris, Myra, and Dakota—had decided to make a pact to set each other up on dates. Blind dates, friend dates, dates of some sort. So they could all find their happily ever afters, or at least a good time. Somehow, my brother had ended up in the middle of it, although Cross had been an accidental blind date. It seemed to have worked for him and Hazel, though, because they were happy and talking about marriage."

I knew Paris was up next, but it had been a good six

months since they'd started this. I didn't realize that she was still on the chopping block.

"Do you have a date?"

She cursed under her breath, and I held back a smile. "Apparently, they're setting me up again."

"Again?"

"Okay, this is the friendship zone. Once I leave here, we're going back to being coworkers. Okay?"

"You said friendship. I'm going to take that as a win."

She glared at me, but I saw her mouth twitching. "I think this is my fifth blind date. I suck at it."

I shook my head, not even bothering to wince. "You don't suck at it. People all over the world suck at dating. I don't understand blind dates at all."

"Seriously?"

"Meeting up with a stranger and then forcing yourself to parade around on a date when you're starting from scratch? No, that doesn't sound like a cup of tea to me. And statistics are going to show that there's not a high success rate."

"My statistics show there is *no* success rate," she said dryly.

"Perhaps, but you're trying. Though you did pale a bit there. What's wrong with your date?"

"Oh, they just helped me set it up. It's tonight. Yay."

This time, I did wince at her tone. "It can't be that bad."

She snorted. "Oh, honey. You have no idea."

And then I smiled, and she smiled back, and something inside me warmed a bit.

Okay, that was interesting. However, it meant nothing.

After all, we were working together, though I was pretty sure Paris didn't like me at all. She may be friends with my group, but she was going on a blind date, and I was in a semi-serious relationship.

And Allison wouldn't like the fact that I had images of Paris in my head. Oh, she wouldn't have minded in the past, but now that Paris and I were working together? No, that wasn't about to happen.

"We'll make this work, Paris."

"My dating, or what?"

I laughed.

"We'll make this whole work thing work. I want this job, and you say you're the best, so let's prove those who think otherwise wrong."

"Maybe," she said softly. "Or perhaps it's only going to get worse."

"We'll make this work," I repeated.

"I sure hope so. Because I love my job. It's pretty much the only thing I have." And with that comment, she walked away, leaving the door open and me standing there wondering what the hell had just happened.

The only thing she had? No, she had more than that. Like I did.

At least, I thought so.

As I looked around my empty office, I wondered what the hell we were going to do. Because I still had a feeling that Paris didn't like me. Not because I was me, but maybe because I represented everything that sucked in this industry. Or perhaps she really didn't like me. I didn't know. But in the end, it wouldn't matter. Because I was going to prove that I was the best at my job. We were going to finish a fucking amazing project. Then, I was going to leave and go back to my previous position and another project that I loved.

And Paris would just have to deal with that.

I had a contract that I was pretty much going to love as long as I could make this work, a woman that I could maybe see myself with someday, and a family I cared for and loved being with.

My life was on the right track, finally.

What could go wrong?

Chapter 2

Paris

I SET MY VODKA GIMLET DOWN NEXT TO MY WATER and smiled at the man in front of me. Was it a smile? Yes, it had to be a smile. It certainly could not be an actual grimace, even though I felt it. Because despite this being my fifth blind date in a matter of six months, I would not grimace at the man who sat across from me.

This one was going to work. I would find something in common with him. I would smile, I would have a wonderful evening and perhaps plan a second date.

This one was not going to end in catastrophic failure.

He licked his lips and grinned at me, but not at my face. No, he was looking at my boobs.

Or maybe I was only imagining things.

Okay, perhaps this date *would* be a catastrophic failure, but that was fine. Nothing was on fire yet. I was not stressing out.

Was I speaking quickly, even in my head? I felt like I was rambling.

I resisted the urge to rub my temples. That wouldn't help anyone. I needed to focus and be happy. And, apparently, take what I could get.

Andy smiled again and reached for his Woodford on ice. It was a good whiskey, one I liked when I traveled, so at least he had decent taste.

"So, what is it you do again? I know you told me the title, but could you maybe tell me a bit more?"

Step one, get to know Andy. Get to know his work. Try not to roll my eyes when he condescended. Not that he would. Just because I'd thought he had been condescending to me right off the bat didn't mean that was actually the case. Perhaps I was putting my own spin on things after my frustrating day at work.

"I'm a hedge fund manager," he said, smiling again, this time, at my eyes. That was a plus.

"Yes, you said that. I don't have a hedge fund or anything like that, so I'd love to hear more about what you do."

I wouldn't. However, I was grasping for straws here. I couldn't bring out my checklist of *okay what are your hobbies, have you been married before, do you condone cheating, what do you think about monogamy, what are your feelings on misogyny, how many children do you want, do you want any children, what is your favorite ice cream topping, do you believe that healthcare should be affordable for all, who did you vote for in the last election?*

Those were all questions that ran through my mind every time I sat down with a new date. Many more issues piled up, too, but I couldn't start off like that while just getting to know him.

Next time I went on a blind date, maybe I'd have him fill out a questionnaire first.

I tapped the table with a finger as he droned on about what he did and how much money he made, and wondered what kind of stationery I would use for that questionnaire. Or would it be electronic? I wasn't sure if I wanted to go fully digital, even though I could probably figure out exactly how to do that and even have it populate a database I could query. It was what I did, after all. Hmm, maybe an app would be best for this. Yes. There were dating apps all over the place, but what if there was an app that got you *through* those awkward dates? Recorded answers to the questions that were going to be complete *hell nos*. That way, more people like me wouldn't have to sit drinking vodka gimlets, pretending to listen when their dates droned on about how their meal partners wouldn't understand but they'd give it a try.

That was fine, some guys got nervous and started to talk like women weren't worth much in the brain department. I would figure this out.

Or I would stress myself out while thinking about it. This wasn't the worst first date I had been on in the past six months, so I figured I'd make the most of it.

"That's so interesting," I lied. Hell, my heart wasn't in this, and even though the light didn't dim in his eyes, I still felt like a heel. I needed to at least seem interested when I spoke to him. It wasn't his fault that I'd had a terrible day at work.

"Enough about me for now," Andy said, smiling. "What about you?" He was quite handsome. Maybe I was actively looking for negatives. The fact that he had asked me what I did and wanted to know more about it had to mean something, didn't it?

"I'm a software quality insurance engineer."

"So, you develop software?"

I shook my head at the common misconception. "No, I test it against the business specifications. Make sure it does everything that the company needs it to in the way it needs to be done. Look for those little things that the average person wouldn't think to check. Everything that you see out there needs to be tested, and the code needs to be combed through. Someone needs to find the bugs before the public does. Before it can fail and possibly end up hurting the bottom line."

"Fascinating. So, you pretty much tell people what they did wrong."

I snorted, not exactly the hottest thing ever, but whatever. "Sometimes it sure does feel like that," I said, shaking my head.

"Though not always. My goal is to be able to work with my team, stay on target with deadlines, and figure things out rather than being the one to call things out all the time." It didn't always work out that way. I had no idea how it was going to work with Prior, though that wasn't something I wanted to focus on right now because thinking about Prior sent me down bad thought paths.

Mostly because I had been attracted to him from the get-go.

The fact that he had a girlfriend, and I was working with him, meant that he was completely off-limits now, in many ways.

Plus, there was just something about him that got under my skin and put my back up. And because of that, I acted like a total jerk.

I didn't like acting that way. I preferred to have true reasons for the things I did. Being confrontational because I was angry about something else meant that I was not acting in my own best interests—and being plain rude. And despite what others said, that wasn't my favorite thing.

"It's good to have people like you around," Andy said, smiling. "I mean, without you, we'd never know when we were doing something wrong. Though it must take a big man to be able to realize that he's wrong. You know what I mean?"

"Sometimes. It's not always about being wrong. It's about finding the bugs that they can't see because they're looking at things differently, or working on so many other things. You should always have a second set of eyes—or even a fifth set—on certain things. Everybody uses software products differently."

"Maybe. And maybe that's too many cooks in the kitchen, you know?"

"Perhaps. But sometimes you need all the help you can get."

"But maybe the guy doesn't want to constantly hear that he's wrong. Can't make for the greatest work environment, can it?"

That was the second time he placed a man in the developer position.

Yes, the last few people I had worked with *had* been men, but that wasn't always the case. I wasn't going to touch on that subject though, because this was a date, and

I didn't need to get into office politics. I had enough of that at work as it was.

And every time that I hung out with my friends, I was probably going to see Prior, and that would just bring more of that nonsense into every part of my life—not something I truly wanted to fixate on.

"Anyway, enough about work," he said casually, taking another sip of his drink. We had ordered a bit ago, but this place was notorious for being slow. It annoyed me from a sustainability and efficiency standpoint, but this was a good place for dates because there was less time shoveling food into your mouth, and more time to get to know one another. At least, usually.

"Anyway, I'm thrilled that Myra set us up."

"How do you know Myra anyway?" he asked.

"We've been friends for a while now. She grew up with one of my college friends, and we all sort of clicked."

"I see. Well, Myra does come from good stock, so any friend of hers is a friend of mine."

Stock. As in *breeding*. This was going to be a fun night.

"Oh?" I asked, trying not to sound like I wanted to hit him.

"You know how it is. Families beget families and all that. Her family's been after her to marry for a while. It's too bad that she and I never clicked. It would have been good for everybody if we had found our way to be with one another. But we just didn't suit."

And now I was second best? The consolation prize? Who exactly did he think I was? What family did he think I came from?

He was sorely mistaken if he thought I ran in the same circles that Myra and Hazel did. My circles weren't even in the same stratosphere as theirs. Mine were more in line with Dakota's background—not that my friends had ever once made me think or feel like I was less because I didn't come from money.

I hadn't come from anything. No, I came from pain, and heartache, and bruises, and screams.

I had come from a trailer park that'd tried its best to fit into every stereotype you could think of. I hadn't come from the same family ties that Myra and Hazel did. And it never once bothered me that I hadn't. However, I had a feeling if the man in front of me ever found out where I really came from, he wouldn't be sitting here in front of me.

I had the nice shoes, the good clothes with the perfect cuts to showcase the curves that I wanted or the business that I needed to do. I knew how to dress to impress, and I used my brain to get where I was.

And maybe my attitude, as well. I didn't care that people called me a bitch. I got where I was because I worked hard and I didn't take any shit. Nor did I let closed doors stop me.

I went to school, got scholarships, got a fantastic fucking degree. And then I got one of the highest paying jobs in my field. I wanted more, and I would get it. That was all part of my life plan.

However, another part of that should be sitting in front of me right now.

Because despite all evidence to the contrary, I didn't like being alone.

I wanted a husband. I wanted a family. I wanted the next stage for the woman who had it all.

However, I had a feeling that Andy was not going to be a part of that.

So that meant I was over five when it came to blind date tries.

Just like I was oh-for-countless-other-times when it came to dating in general.

I shouldn't be surprised.

We were all trying to find men that suited us, but maybe the problem with our whole pact was that we didn't know any men that suited us personally. So, how could we find men that suited our friends?

Maybe I was thinking too hard and being too cynical about everything.

"Do your parents summer with Myra's?" he asked, and I pulled myself out of my thoughts.

"No, my parents are dead."

A complete lie, but I was used to saying it in harsh tones like I had right then.

So harsh, in fact, that he blanched a bit, blinked, and then smiled, even though it didn't reach his eyes.

"My condolences."

"It's been a long time," I said, compounding on the lie.

No one needed to know where my parents were now. I didn't want to think about them at all.

No one needed to think about them.

"I take it your family summers with Myra's?"

"Sometimes. They used to summer more with the parents of your other friend, Hazel."

"Ah," I said, not sure where to go with that.

"It was so sad when they passed. Even sadder when Hazel cut ties with her former husband. His family was quite influential."

"Well, the whole kidnapping and drugging and murder part of the whole situation probably put a downer on summer vacations," I said casually, taking a sip of my gimlet.

His cheeks reddened. This time, there was more of a snarl on his lips.

"Things like that do tend to tarnish things, don't they?

"And I would assume the screaming and the bleeding and the gunshots probably tarnished things a bit more."

"Paris," he admonished.

"What? Hazel's ex was an asshole. And if you're sad that you can't go to the country club with his family anymore, that's on you, not her."

"I'm just saying, using your words nicely would be more beneficial in these things. If you would only tell me what she did to push him, then perhaps we could come to an understanding. What drove him over the edge? Why didn't she listen to him to begin with?"

Andy was very lucky that I did not want to waste good vodka by throwing my drink in his face. Instead, I took another sip and pushed back from the table.

"You know what? Thank you for this evening, because you showed me what I've been missing on the other side of the table."

"Excuse me?" he asked, his voice icy and clipped.

"It shows me that I should just give up dating altogether. Especially if you are what's out there."

"You cannot say that to me. You don't know who I am. My family."

"I think I know *exactly* who you are. Have a wonderful night, Andy." I put two twenties on the table.

"Since I didn't eat, I bet you can take the rest home to your mother. Or whoever else is part of your *inner circle*."

I started to storm past him, but he stood up abruptly and pushed past me. His shoulder shoved into mine, and I staggered a bit, making a scene as I clutched the table to steady myself.

And then, as if the heavens had opened up, an angel— or perhaps the devil himself—came to my side and gripped my elbow.

"Paris?"

I turned, mortification sliding over me as I tilted my head, hoping to hell my face wasn't as red as it felt.

I put on that icy façade that had gotten me through so much.

The bitch queen. The ice queen. The one that everybody thought probably went down on her knees to get where she was in her job. All the things they whispered about me and had for so many years. It all slid over my skin, and I became the Paris that others sneered at. The one they didn't look down on because they didn't do anything but fear and admire her.

"Prior," I said, my voice smooth and silky.

"Are you okay?"

"I've been better," I said, embarrassment still acute. I knew he had to have seen it. I was good at hiding most things, but it was getting harder and harder to hide it all today.

"Do I need to go after him and hurt him?" he asked, his voice low.

We were standing at the edge of the tables near the wall, so people were now turned away, focusing on their dinners. Thank God.

"No, he's not worth it. I'll make sure that Myra knows that, too."

He looked over my head, frowning. He'd cut his beard a bit and had smoothed back his hair since I saw him that morning. I couldn't help but wonder why. He had always been handsome, but now he looked even more so.

I was losing my mind.

"I'm sorry," he whispered.

"Don't be. Another blind date to put in the trash. I should go, though."

"I was heading to the bar for a drink. Join me?"

I shook my head. "I should call an Uber, and I've already had one drink."

"Don't let him win," Prior said, his voice low.

I let out a sigh and took Prior's elbow as we walked towards the bar.

"Hopefully, I left enough money for the waitress," I whispered, looking over to where they were cleaning up the empty table. They hadn't even brought our food.

Prior gestured towards the bartender as we took our seats and then helped me onto the bar stool.

"You didn't see it, but that man—I'm not going to call him your date—the asshole put down a few more twenties. The waitress will be covered. And I'm pretty sure they didn't even start on your food yet since this place takes like three hours to do anything," he whispered under his breath, and I held back a laugh.

"So, what are we having?" the bartender asked as he put two cocktail napkins in front of us.

"A vodka gimlet? Gray Goose?"

"You've got it," he said, looking at Prior.

"Make that two," he said, and then the bartender was off, working on our order.

"You like gimlets?"

"I like Gray Goose. And whatever makes it easy for the bartender, I'm up for it. You okay getting home on your own?" he asked, studying my face.

I hated that he was so kind to me. That he had witnessed any of what had just happened.

"I'm fine, like always. Annoyed that I let him get under my skin, but whatever."

"What did he do?"

"I don't want to get into it, but let's just say he knew Hazel's ex."

Prior's gaze darkened, and his jaw tightened. Considering that his brothers had been shot because of that man, I didn't blame Prior for the anger.

"You should have let me punch him."

"Let's not make a scene. More than I already did," I said as the bartender put our drinks down. Prior held his up and clinked my glass in a weak toast.

"To that sixth blind date," he said, smiling.

I rolled my eyes and then took a sip of my drink. "Let's not talk about that. I'm the worst at dating."

"I'm not the best at it either, though I think I'm learning," Prior said, his voice casual.

"From what I hear, you and Allison have been together for a few months now. I guess you're much better at it than you think."

Prior shrugged.

"Maybe it just takes finding the right person."

I ignored the clutch in my heart at that. Not that I wanted Prior, because that was a big hell no. It was more that he seemed happy, he had found that person.

And I hadn't.

Jealousy? Oh, I hated that.

"I may have to give up this whole dating thing."

Prior's brows rose. "Maybe you're waiting for the prince after a bunch of frogs?"

"There's that whole meme where the prince is dumb and stuck in a tree or something, and the princess needs to go find him. Sometimes I feel like that's me."

Prior laughed, shaking his head, and I took another sip of my drink, finally feeling a bit calmer.

Andy hadn't been good for me from the start. I had a feeling, no...I knew from the bottom of my heart that Myra had no idea of his true nature. Because the guy had seemed sweet, but apparently, he was as cold as a snake.

I would tell Myra, but hopefully, she would know that it wasn't her fault and I didn't blame her.

"Thank you for making me laugh," I said. "I needed this."

"Anytime."

I shook my head, pulling myself out of my self-pity. "Wait, why are you here? Are you stalking me?"

"Not at all. I'm here to meet Allison." He checked his phone. "She should be here any minute now. For her, being on time means being about fifteen minutes late. I'm used to it."

"That would drive me up the wall," I said, shaking my head.

"You get used to it." There was real warmth in his eyes.

Damn, there was that little bit of jealousy again. I must want to be with someone.

We started talking some more about work, and I finally relaxed. And then when a well-manicured hand slid up to Prior's shoulder, we both jumped.

It wasn't guilt; more like we had been so into our conversation that we had completely forgotten everyone and everything else.

Crap.

"Prior?" a cool voice asked. "Who's this?"

And that reminded me that over the past six months they had been together, he'd never once brought Allison to our group meals or activities. We didn't do them as often as maybe Hazel would have liked, but I hung out with Prior enough.

Weird.

"Hey. This is Paris, a friend of Hazel's. She had a shitty date, so I was making sure she was okay while I waited for you."

He leaned forward and kissed Allison on the cheek and then wrapped his arm around her waist.

"Allison, Paris. Paris, Allison."

"It's nice to meet you. Thanks for letting me borrow him while I got over my stupor. Have a great dinner."

"Of course. I'm glad that you had a wonderful time with my Prior."

I didn't miss the possessiveness.

From the outside looking in, it did look a bit shady, and I didn't blame her for that.

"You guys have a good dinner. I'm headed home." I reached for my purse, but Prior shook his head.

"I've got this."

I didn't miss the narrowing of Allison's eyes, but Prior did.

I shook my head again.

"Nope. I've got it. Check on your table, and I will get an Uber. Thank you again," I said, keeping my voice professional.

When Allison tugged him away, Prior stared at me, then gave me a tight nod before leaving.

If I were honest with myself, I probably would have reacted the same as Allison had. Because it did look wrong from an outsider's point of view. I'd have to apologize to her if I ever saw her again.

However, now I needed to go home. I was going to run a nice bubble bath, drink some tea, and pretend like I had my life in order.

Because honestly, I knew that I didn't.

And no matter how many life plans I made, nothing would change until I figured out how to fix it myself.

Chapter 3

Prior

IF I'D THOUGHT MY JOB WOULD GET EASIER AFTER watching Benji walk away after Paris had scolded him my first day on the job, I was insanely wrong.

In fact, it felt like I had been thrown into the middle of a war zone, and I didn't exactly know how it had happened.

"If you have a problem with the way that I'm doing things, talk to me to my face rather than behind my back," Paris's voice echoed into my office, and I rubbed my temple.

I honest to God did not blame her for raising her voice. In fact, she wasn't actually yelling. She was merely trying to explain to Benji and the others what the fuck was wrong.

However, the people that worked in this branch seemed to have it out for her.

And if I tried to stand up for her, she'd probably bite my head off. She did not need me to do that. What she needed was for me to get my work done.

However, it was difficult when I knew I wouldn't be alone in my office in five minutes or less.

As footsteps came towards me, I realized it had been less than five minutes...by a lot.

"Can you fucking believe her?" Benji mumbled under his breath and closed the door behind him.

I raised a brow and simply stared at the man. "I'm in the middle of something. Do you need something from me?"

Benji's eyes widened as if he were confused as to why I would be annoyed that someone would interrupt me during a fucking workday.

"What? Didn't you just hear what she said to me?"

"This is not high school, Benji. We're working. You had a huge bug in your code, and she happened to find it. That's her job. What's with you?"

"It's her tone."

"If she was a man, would you be saying the same thing?" And here I was, standing up for her. But, fuck. It would be wrong if I kicked him out without saying what I thought.

I was pretty sure that Paris couldn't even hear me through the walls, so it wasn't like she could get angry with me about it. Well, she probably could. She'd likely find a way. However, I did not blame her for what she'd said to Benji. Not in the least.

"You need to lay off," I continued, my voice as calm as possible. "Don't you hear how you sound?"

"I don't know why everyone has to bring up the fact that she's a woman. I'd hate the way she's acting towards me if she was a man."

"Okay. That's fine. However, you need to watch the way you speak."

"I thought you'd be on my side," Benji grumbled. Before I could say anything, he slammed out of my office, and I closed my eyes.

"Jesus," I whispered.

"I see you're having as good a day as I am," I heard and looked up to see Paris standing in my now-open doorway.

"How did you open the door without me noticing?" I asked, and she rolled her eyes.

"You know me. I'm just, you know, a secret spy or something. Seriously, though, you had your eyes closed and were rubbing your temples."

"Sorry about that," I said.

"No need to apologize to me." She paused and looked over her shoulder before closing the door behind her.

"Sorry about Benji," I said.

"It's getting worse," she said, beginning to pace my office.

"I know it is. And in case you were wondering, I did tell him to knock it off while he was in here."

She paused and looked at me, then tilted her head. "You know, for some reason, I actually figured you'd defend me. Even though I don't need you to do that."

I resisted the urge to roll my eyes. "Well, considering I was thinking pretty much the exact thing you just said, I'm going to count that as a win."

She paused.

"What do you mean?"

"Let's go get some lunch," I said suddenly, standing up from behind my desk. It was lunchtime, and while I might have brought something to eat, I needed to get out of this office. There was something wrong here. And, frankly, I needed help with my project, something that would take time and brainpower.

"You want to go to lunch? With me?" she asked, her voice deadpan.

"Why wouldn't I?"

"Because I'm the Shark? And nobody on this floor likes to eat lunch with me."

I narrowed my eyes, rage at the rest of the people in this building filling me up once again.

"That's going to change. We're friends, Paris. We can go to lunch. Notice I didn't say *take you to* lunch."

She rolled her eyes, her lips twitching into a smile. "So, I take it you're not going to be chivalrous and pay, then?"

"Hey, I'm pretty sure you once said that chivalry is dead, and you were glad of it."

"I did not. But I like to open doors for some people if I get there first."

"See? Chivalry. And it doesn't matter. I'm not paying for your lunch because then you'll get all huffy and think that I am trying to take care of you, when I'm clearly not. I'm just hungry, and you happen to be here."

She laughed, shaking her head.

"I have no idea what to believe right now."

"I don't either. Which is a good thing. Either way, come on, let's go get something to eat."

"And you don't care that others will think that I'm sleeping with you because I'm going out to eat with you?" she asked, not moving away from the door. I paused as I slid my phone into my pocket.

"Well, I have a steady girlfriend, and most of the

people in this department know that. If they're going to think that I'm cheating as well as sleeping with someone I work with, then that's on them." I paused. "However, if it's going to be too much for you, let me know. I'm in a position where I can say *fuck it* and we can let them think what they want, but you might not be."

"You're right." She ran her hands down her face, letting out a breath. "I'm overthinking this because Benji pissed me off once again. As it is, we've been in your office with the door closed for a little too long. They probably think I'm giving you a blowjob or something." Her eyes widened, and she put her hand over her mouth before mumbling, "I didn't say that. Please don't send me to HR."

I threw back my head and laughed, shaking my head. "Seriously, we're friends. And friends don't give each other blowjobs."

"That's good to know. Either way, I'm sorry. I'm just pissed off, and it makes me say things I shouldn't. I'm glad it's with you and not someone who would report me for saying something completely inappropriate."

"Come on, let's get you something to eat."

"Are you sure? I saw you bring your little lunchbox in with you."

"Ouch. Ha-ha. I did. Now, I'm in the mood for whatever's closest. Lead the way, you're the expert here when it comes to places to go."

"I have no idea if you're being sarcastic or not," she said, narrowing her eyes.

"Shut up," I said and opened the door, gesturing for her to lead the way. Nobody paid us any mind, and Benji was the only one who glared. I had a feeling this was mostly Benji acting up and not anyone else. And that was something I needed to think about. Or that was something Paris *and* I would have to deal with. I let her lead the way because I was done stepping on her toes. I seemed to do that enough when it came to her.

We ended up at a little café near work, and I smiled as Paris looked around, not quite judging but taking things in.

"Do you feel like we're cheating on Dakota's place?" I asked, my voice a whisper.

"A little," she said, her cheeks blushing a bit.

"If we were closer to that place during our lunch break, you know I'd be there in a heartbeat. I like Dakota's place. I like Dakota."

Her eyes narrowed a little. "What do you mean by that?"

I held my hands up in protest. "Hey, just that I like Dakota. I like all of you guys. It's nice having all of Hazel's friends as part of our crew. That's all I was saying. Dakota is a nice woman, and I like her kid."

"Okay, sorry. I'm a little overprotective when it comes to my friends."

"Shocking," I said, and she rolled her eyes at me before she stabbed her salad with her fork.

I mixed mine up, even as I watched the way she ate hers in little pieces. I held back a smile at that. If I could coat everything with dressing and mix it all up so I got a little bit of each thing in every bite, I would. And would be happy. Paris seemed to like things one at a time.

That was probably why I developed things, and she broke them apart and tested them out.

Or maybe I was thinking a little too hard on all that shit.

"So now that we're out of the building, you doing okay?" I asked. I could have slapped myself for asking.

All the easy camaraderie we had established fizzled like a balloon being popped.

"It's just normal work stuff. I think Benji has a burr up his butt, even though me doing my job doesn't reflect on him at all. He liked your predecessor about four people ago, and they were good friends."

"Seriously? I didn't know that."

"Yep. When that guy was let go, though we didn't know he'd been fired, Benji took it personally."

"And...he blamed you."

"He either blamed me because I was the one testing

the software, or because I'm a woman. Or maybe he simply doesn't like me. I don't know, but I had nothing to do with it. I don't even know why the guy was fired. It's none of my business. My job is to get the work done and try to enjoy what I do. And despite Benji and the *Shark* comments that he likes to spread around, I do like my job."

"That's good. I don't know if I could like a job where I had to be on guard all the time."

"Considering you're only visiting our branch for six months and you're going to be the new guy for a while, I would assume you'd also feel on guard."

I shrugged before taking another bite of my salad. "I'm used to fitting in where I need to. And if I don't, I make do."

"That must be nice."

I shook my head, smiling. "Sometimes. And other times, I'm the loud, annoying brother that my siblings make fun of. It works. We all find our places."

"Maybe. Or perhaps we're stuck in this egocentric, esoteric world where we don't know where we are, and we're left to an existential crisis."

"That was a lot of big words, and I'm very confused now," I said, laughing.

"Well, I try." She smiled then, her eyes brightening. I liked it when she smiled like that, it meant that it actually hit her, rather than her pretending in order to make everybody feel better.

My phone buzzed, and I looked down at the readout, smiling again.

"You mind if I take this real quick?" I asked, and Paris shook her head. I answered, pulling back from the table so I could go outside and not annoy everybody with my phone call.

"Hey there, babe," I said, walking out of the building. I noticed Paris staring at me as I did. I waved before standing right outside the glass windows. Our table was right on the other side of the windowpane, and if I talked loudly enough, I had a feeling that Paris would be able to hear everything I said. Not a big deal, I just didn't want the whole building annoyed by me talking on the phone.

"Hey there, love."

Love? Since when did she call me *love?* We weren't quite at the whole love stage, at least I didn't think so. Neither of us had said it, and while I was enjoying our time together, I wasn't ready to take the next step. I might joke a lot, but I was actually slow in determining certain aspects of what I wanted.

That might not be the best reaction for most people, but it usually worked for me.

"I'm on a lunch break, what's up?"

"I was hoping you were on your lunch break. You

brought your own, right? Or did you want to meet up quick?" she asked, her voice warm.

"I brought my own, but I ended up needing to take a coworker out for lunch. Kind of a bad day, so we decided to get out of the office and breathe for a bit. My salad is fucking good, though."

"Oh? I wish I had known that. I could have met up with you guys."

"Sorry, it all happened kinda fast. We're still on for dinner tonight, right?" I asked.

"Yes. Well, give Benji my love. Or at least tell him hi." She laughed. "Got to go. Talk to you soon. Bye, babe."

"Bye," I said to silence. She had already disconnected.

I hadn't had a chance to correct her, and now I felt like a heel. Even though Paris and I were just friends, and there was nothing romantic between us at all, Allison didn't like Paris. She didn't like the fact that I hung out with women at all. And she didn't like that she had been late to our date, only to show up and see Paris and me having a drink together. Later, she had yelled, ranted, and I had apologized. It had probably looked bad from the outside, but I hated the fact that she didn't trust me.

So, it was my job to make sure that whatever I did now, she could trust me at all times.

I shook my head, stuck my phone into my pocket, and went back inside to finish my salad.

"Allison?" Paris asked.

"Yes."

"Is she upset that we're eating lunch together?" At my look, she continued. "She wasn't a huge fan of me from what I could tell after our impromptu drink that night."

"Ah," I began. "No, she wasn't too happy."

"I don't know if I blame her. It did look pretty bad for you."

"The fact that she thinks I'm with Benji for lunch right now is probably not going to be any better. I'll have to correct her assumption later."

Paris narrowed her eyes. "Why didn't you tell her?" she asked, glaring at me.

"Because she assumed and then hung up before I could correct her. I didn't want to get into a fight over the phone. I should have corrected her, and I will. That's on me. I swear, nothing hinky is going on."

"Oh, I know nothing hinky is going on, considering I'm the one telling you that. But now she's going to think you're cheating on her with me, and I'm going to be the bad guy."

"No," I said, angry now. "She'll be fine. She just gets jealous over every single little fucking thing," I growled out. "And I didn't want to get into it over the phone. But I will set things right as soon as I see her tonight. Promise."

"As long as she doesn't come and try to like...slice my tires or something."

"Allison's not like that," I said, and Paris sighed.

"No, but she's going to be hurt, and that'll be on me as much as you."

"You're right. Fuck." I pinched the bridge of my nose. "I handled that wrong."

"Yes, you did."

I looked down at my salad and then pushed it away, shaking my head. "I can't eat anymore. Now I'm just pissed off at myself."

"You can fix it."

"I will. But I need to get back."

"Me, too. I'm done anyway."

"Sorry this lunch turned out to be a bust," I said.

"I ate, and I got to yell at you, I'm going to count that as a bonus."

I rolled my eyes, and we went back to work. Benji wasn't in the office since he was on his lunch break. I counted that as a win because I wasn't in the mood to deal with anything else right now.

By the time we got back to our desks, I was pissed off at myself and quickly shot off a text.

Me: *By the way, I was out to lunch with Paris today, not Benji. Didn't correct you on the phone before you hung up. Sorry about that, babe.*

Allison: *What?*

Me: *She had a shitty day, and I needed to get out too. We each paid for our own meal, but I didn't correct you. I'm sorry.*

Allison was quiet for long enough that I had a feeling I had made a big fucking mistake. Allison always blew everything out of proportion, and I really didn't want to deal with it over the phone just then.

I shouldn't have lied by omission, though. Fuck.

Allison: *I get it. I shouldn't have figured it was a man right off the bat. You work with women too. Hope you had a good lunch. I'll see you tonight?*

I blinked, wondering exactly what had just happened.

Me: *I'll see you then.*

Allison: *Sounds good, babe.*

And then she didn't say anything else. I blinked, wondering exactly what had just happened.

I shook my head, put my phone away, and went back to work. It had been a long time since I'd had a serious girlfriend. And I'd never had one who tended to get as jealous as Allison did. Maybe I was overreacting.

Or perhaps I needed to get my head out of my ass and get back to work. I could deal with my problems with Allison and whatever I was feeling later. Because I had no idea if I loved my girlfriend. And considering that we had been together as long as we had? That was a fucking problem. It didn't have anything to do with the work in front of me at the moment, though. The project I needed to focus on.

By the time I was ready to knock off for the day, my mind was clear, and I was fucking proud of the work I had accomplished.

We were getting far on this project, and I was happy to see where we were headed. I couldn't wait to see what Paris thought about it, because she could always pick apart the pieces that I was having trouble with and sometimes get me back on the right track—or even a better one. Even if I didn't always think those were the problem areas to begin with. That was what a team was for.

I packed up my stuff, including the lunch I hadn't eaten, then made my way to the front where Paris happened to be, as well.

I raised a brow, and she rolled her eyes.

"Why are we on the same schedule today?" I asked her.

"Because it's my schedule. Therefore, it's the best schedule," Paris said, and I laughed. I didn't miss the way Benji narrowed his eyes at us.

Fuck, it was going to be fun working out the rest of my contract if this was how Benji was going to act.

"You ready to head out?" I asked, and Paris nodded.

"Let's get to it," she said and turned away from Benji,

even though I knew she had seen the glare he'd shot us. There was nothing we could do about it. It was something that would have to be taken care of soon, though.

We made our way towards the parking lot, and Paris's shoulders stiffened as she looked around.

The hairs on the back of my neck stood on end, and I frowned, looking around with her.

"What is it?" I asked.

"I don't know. It felt like someone was watching me." She looked towards the building, and I followed her gaze. We didn't see anyone in the windows.

"Think I'm losing my mind. Tough day."

"You okay getting home?" I asked, my gaze peeled for any danger. Ever since the attack on Hazel and my brothers, I didn't take my safety for granted anymore.

She shook her head. "I'm fine. I think I'm just tired."

I nodded, searching her face. I didn't see any lies in what she'd said. "Drive safe," I said.

"You too. And work things out with Allison," she said, and I nodded.

"I already texted her, and she said it was fine."

Her brows rose. "Oh?"

"Yep. It turns out I'm an asshole, but at least I'm a truthful one."

She snorted and then got into her car, waving as she did.

"Thanks for being a good man."

"I'm trying," I said, and then got into my own vehicle, waiting for her to pull away before I did.

I didn't like that she'd felt like someone was watching her, but I hoped that we were sensing things that weren't there. After all, we'd been through enough. And considering that we'd had a hard workday, it could just be that.

It couldn't be anything else.

At least, I hoped to hell it wasn't.

Chapter 4

Paris

THIS TIME, I WAS GOING TO MAKE OUR PLAN WORK.
Dakota had promised me that the man was sweet, wasn't a
condescending asshole, and was an excellent tipper. The
fact that we were now at the bottom of the barrel when it
came to men we had met in our lives, just told me that this
was going to work.

Why?

Because, honestly, there wasn't another alternative. It
was either the date in front of me or find an app to find
partners for one another. And while a few people in my
life had done that, and said it had worked out or at least

they hadn't turned into a bleeding ball of fire, none of us really wanted to do that. Honestly, it wasn't what we were trying for. Our goal was to find dates for each other.

And that meant not going on an app and swiping or clicking or loving or hoping a hookup was inevitable.

And although I missed sex, and a hookup would be nice, I wasn't ready for that.

No, what I wanted was a *connection*.

Honestly, I didn't think that was going to happen anytime soon.

I tossed that thought from my head, annoyed with myself. It really wouldn't happen if all I did was complain about it.

I pushed those thoughts away and smiled at my date.

The man seemed like a nice guy. I was going to count that as a blessing. We were sitting at a little Mediterranean restaurant that I had been to a couple of times before because the naan they served at the beginning was twice the size of my head and came with the best olive oil and feta cheese with seasonings dip ever.

"I love this place," I said to my date, grinning. "Have you been here before, Kansas?" I asked.

Yes, his name was Kansas. And my friend Dakota had introduced me to him. All of us had thought Dakota should have been the one going out with him for the name thing alone, but she had pushed him my way. She thought we would be good together. I figured it was because it wasn't her turn and she didn't want to have anything to do with dating.

For a group of women who had gone into this wanting to find a connection with someone, we sure were hesitant when it came to the actual dating part.

Probably because of how everything had started with Hazel. But again, I didn't want my thoughts to go down that path, so I focused on Kansas.

He had dark blue eyes behind wire-rimmed glasses. His spiky hair was thinning a little bit at the corners, but that didn't bother me at all. I was probably losing about as much hair as he was at my age.

It honestly made him look more regal.

He had a soft smile, a firm jaw, and was pretty built.

What I liked beyond the looks that gave me warm feelings was that he had already made me laugh once when he met me in front of the building. It had been some stupid joke about parking, but it had made me laugh, and I counted that as a win.

See? Tonight was already going better than the last date I'd been on. And he wasn't connected to any murders that I knew of.

I should probably throw salt over my shoulder or knock on wood if I was going to state things like that in my head.

"I've been here once. I liked the kabobs." He smiled again, a little blush right under his wire frames. I warmed, leaning in. That was cute. Only...why was he blushing?

He must've seen the look on my face because he turned even redder. "Sorry. I usually just end up cooking at home or ordering in Panda Express or a hamburger."

I shrugged, shaking my head. "Why would you be embarrassed about that?"

"Because your name is Paris. And look at you. You're all cosmopolitan, and you probably go out to eat at fancy places like this all the time."

I didn't think this place was all that fancy, but I guessed it was, compared to fast food. This restaurant was quite reasonable compared to some of the other restaurants in Boulder. I didn't say that, though. Instead, I smiled. "I don't think I'm anywhere close to cosmopolitan. I haven't even been to my namesake."

His eyes widened. "For real?"

"I'm a Colorado girl. I've never even been out of the country. And Boulder isn't that cosmopolitan. The mountains right there kind of make it hard," I said, and he smiled at me again. I liked that expression. I could get to appreciate that smile.

"Oh, this place is very cosmo for me. Though I don't even think I've had a cosmo before."

"I've had one because it was all the rage back before I

was legally allowed to drink, thanks to *Sex and the City*. They're a little too bright pink and sweet for me."

"Well, good thing this place is a bring your own bottle establishment, and we can't bring the hard liquor in with us."

"True. But I'm fine with water or iced tea."

"Sounds like a plan to me." The waiter came over and handed out that beautiful naan that smelled so good my mouth started to water. And then he walked away since neither of us was quite ready to order.

"I could probably gorge myself on this naan," he said.

"I was just thinking the same thing," I said with a laugh.

"Although, I was looking at maybe getting a little kibbeh to start with. And then I could probably fall into the chicken shawarma or even a Greek moussaka."

His browse rose. "I was thinking maybe a chicken kabab. I don't know if I'm that adventurous."

"You could taste some of mine. That is if you're not going to be too full from all the naan."

"Oh, I don't share food. As it is, I'm kind of shaking even having to share the naan right now."

I held back a frown.

"I'm sorry. I can ask our waiter to get a second one. Or maybe we can cut it into pieces and get a different plate. I didn't even think about that. I'm sorry."

He shook his head. "No, it's not about germs. Just the *sharing*." He winked. "I share *some* things, but not others."

I held back another frown, wondering where exactly he was going with this. "Oh?"

"You didn't laugh, was my joke not good enough?"

"A joke?" I asked, uneasy all of a sudden. "I'm sorry, I don't get it."

"About the sharing. I mean, that's why we're here tonight. My wife would be here too, but I figured it'd be good for the two of us to get to know each other before you come and meet June. She's excited to get to know you. Like I am. I mean, the fact that she's going to share me with you is going to be kind of fun, isn't it? That *is* what this is, right? Dakota was setting us up so you could join us for an evening or three."

I just blinked at him and swallowed hard. I wondered how the hell I had gotten into this situation.

"You're...married?" I looked down at his left hand and didn't see a ring.

"Oh, well, of course, I am. Didn't Dakota tell you that?"

I tried to be calm, to use my words gently. "I don't think Dakota is aware you're married. You probably never mentioned it. Nor are you wearing a wedding ring." See? I was not hurting anyone. Wasn't screaming. Wasn't running out of the building so quickly there was a Paris-shaped hole in the door.

"Oh, we didn't do wedding rings. We got matching tattoos. And June's nipple rings match my cock ring."

He was saying the words pretty low, but a family of four glared at us from the other table. I sank into my chair, trying to become invisible.

"Oh?"

"Don't tell me you don't like body jewelry. Are you going to judge?" He narrowed his blue eyes behind those wire-framed glasses.

"No, not at all." I shook my head. "I mean, you do you. I like body jewelry and tattoos and everything. And I don't mind people being in polyamorous relationships or triads or anything that makes them happy. Only, I wasn't aware that this was happening."

"Well, shit," Kansas said, shaking his head. "I knew this was too good to be true. June said I should have just brought you over to the house rather than trying to take you somewhere fancy."

"Oh."

There were other words I should probably say, but I didn't have any of them at the moment.

Apparently, blind date number six was an invitation to join an already married couple for a night or three of sex.

I was going to throttle Dakota when next I had a chance.

I took back that word as shivers ran down my back. No, I wasn't going to use violence against her. It wouldn't be good for either of us, but I *was* going to yell. Or get her back somehow. Maybe steal a pastry. Yes, I would steal a pastry. One with tons of sugar and cream cheese and lots of flaky goodness.

"This is embarrassing."

"We only ordered water, so why don't you go? I'll handle the waiter."

He gave me a pleading look, and I shook my head.

"Not going to happen, Kansas."

"You have my number in case you ever want to join June and me. We play Yahtzee on Thursday night, too. And that's not a euphemism. We like to yell out 'Yahtzee' while even playing the game."

He winked, and I still didn't know if that was an actual euphemism or not. And then he left.

And there I was, sitting at my table, looking at his empty seat and my now-cold naan, wondering exactly what I was supposed to do now. Did I leave a tip? Did I pay for the naan even though we hadn't ordered? Did I crawl and hide?

Thankfully, the family of four left before I had a

chance to say anything, but then a shadow covered my table, and I had a horrible feeling.

I looked up and swallowed hard.

"Why are you here?" I asked.

Prior shrugged. "My neighborhood is right behind this place. I come here often. I noticed a man walking away from your table, so I figured I'd see what was up."

"Is there like a candid camera here to watch me have these bad dates? Are you orchestrating it or something?" I asked, rubbing my temples.

"No, but it sounds like you could use a drink."

"I did not BYOB."

He held up a thermal case. "I brought wine."

"You brought wine to sit by yourself?" I asked and then could've slapped myself. "Wait, where's Allison?"

"Allison is at work." He rolled his eyes. "I was stood up. Which is fine. She said she might have to work late, but I figured I'd show up anyway since I'm starving. So, mind if I join you?"

"I'm not having dinner with you while you should be with a girlfriend," I said. There were rules about that sort of thing.

"We're coworkers. Friends. Well...practically."

"Thanks," I said, putting as much sarcasm as I could into my tone.

"Come on. We'll eat. You'll tell me exactly what made

you blush so hard, and I'll make sure I tell Allison what we're doing."

I sighed. Frankly, I was starving and wanted to eat my naan. Even if it was cold, it was delicious anyway.

"Fine, but this is embarrassing."

Prior just shook his head, smiled at me, and then went over to talk to the waiter.

They switched out his water glass, popped open the bottle of wine, and we both ordered our meals quickly. It was as if Kansas had never been there, and I hadn't been utterly embarrassed.

I was sure the waitstaff would be talking about this for a while because it wasn't precisely like Kansas had been quiet. But still, I was exhausted, utterly tired of dating.

Prior frowned as the waiter put fresh naan on the table, but I held up my hand when he tried to take the old naan.

"I'll eat that, too. Please, don't waste food."

He smiled and then walked away, and I dug into the naan, wanting its yummy goodness to make everything better.

I sighed. "I'm done," I mumbled before I even realized I'd said the words.

"Excuse me? You're done with what? Because I'm pretty sure you're not done with that naan," he said, and I resisted the urge to flip him off. I'd already had a bad enough night. I didn't want to get kicked out for vulgarity on top of it all.

"I'm done dating," I said after I swallowed hard. Damn, that naan was good.

"How could it be that bad?"

"First, you're in a stable relationship, so...fuck you." I whispered the last part. "Second, this was not a date. Tonight was an invitation to join his marital bed with his wife. Kansas and June, the cutest polyamorous couple ever." I dug into the naan again, while Prior just sat there, blinking at me. It was good that he didn't laugh, because I was not in the mood.

"Well, that's a new one. I mean, I was standing right there, they could have invited me."

I looked at him and burst out laughing. "Wow, full of yourself, aren't you?"

"I could make a joke that *someone* should be full of *me*, but that's weird," he said, and I closed my eyes, trying not to laugh.

"Please, no sex jokes. We're coworkers."

"That is true. By the way, while you were digging into that naan, I texted Allison, and she said this was fine. I explained about the bad date, though I want to go into detail just so she understands why I'm eating dinner with you."

I waved my hand in the air. "Go ahead. Tell the

world. I don't care. As long as you don't get in trouble for making me feel good." I paused. "I mean...helping me have a better night, not making me feel good. Sexually. And I haven't even had any wine yet."

He held up his glass, and I held up mine, we clinked them before I took a big gulp of the liquid.

"Slow down there, slugger."

"Oh, shush. This is the only glass I'll have. But between this and the food I'm about to indulge in, this is the only good thing to come out of the evening."

"Ouch. I'm sitting right here."

"I'm not taking back my statement," I said, grinning.

"Anyway, thank you," I said after a while. The waiter set our food in front of us, and I groaned, saying my thanks.

Prior leaned forward. "You're welcome. And dear God, this is so much food, but I'm going to eat it all."

"Is it okay if I steal some of yours? The waiter brought an extra plate like we asked."

"Thank God that's why you ordered the extra plate because I wanted to try yours."

"See? I guess we *are* friends."

He winked at me, and I rolled my eyes.

"Took you long enough, but here we are, best friends forever."

"Don't push your luck."

We ate, talked about work, and our friends, and I did my best to push thoughts of Kansas and June out of my head. The waiter picked up our empty plates, and we were looking over the dessert menu when my phone rang.

I had it on Do Not Disturb except for a few people, and I recognized that ring.

Cold sweat covered my body, and Prior stiffened in front of me.

"What is it?"

"Nothing. But I need to answer this."

"Okay. I'm here." I picked up the phone and prayed that everything was okay, but I knew it wasn't going to be.

"Hello?" I asked as I stood up from the table and made my way out the door so no one could overhear me.

"Hello, Paris, it's Detective Buker. I have some news for you."

As he began to speak, my body sagged as I leaned against the post in front of the door. I wondered how in the hell this had happened. It couldn't be happening.

Screams and burns and shouts. Hard slaps and slices. Little voices and cries. It all came back to me, but I didn't tear up. I stood there, shocked, sweat almost pouring down my body.

And when I hung up the phone, I wondered what the hell I was going to do.

And then Prior was there, his hands on my shoulders.

I knew he was saying my name over and over again, even though I couldn't really hear him. It took me a minute, and then I looked up at him and swallowed hard.

"Paris? What is it? Is it one of the girls? Is it Joshua?" he asked, speaking about Dakota's son.

I pulled away, needing space, needing *something*. I didn't know what exactly that was. "No, they're okay. I...I need to go home, though."

"I'm going to drive you."

"No, you can't. Your car is here."

"Let me text my brothers and see what they can do to help me out. You're not driving in this condition."

I nodded, hating that I felt so small, hating the way I didn't have control.

I heard him talking to Macon and Nate. Apparently, they said they would come and get my car and take it to my place. They had the address from Hazel. It was just another way I knew that, somehow, we were all becoming one large group, all the connections so close.

There were things they didn't know about me, things I never wanted them to know. But now it was all coming back.

"Come on, let me get my car. I'll take you home."

"They need the keys," I whispered.

"Macon is pulling in right now. I'll get them to him."

I hadn't even realized that any time had passed. I hadn't even paid my half of the bill.

What was wrong with me?

I couldn't breathe, couldn't think, couldn't do anything.

More time passed, and then Nate was there, and the guys gave me concerned looks. I couldn't focus on them right now, so I ignored them.

And then I was in Prior's car, somehow buckled in and on my way home with Prior. He had such worry on his face that I turned away.

I needed to breathe, needed to think.

Because the man who had killed my sister was out of prison.

The asshole who had tortured me, who still gave me nightmares, who had ruined everything in my life was out.

And I knew it was only a matter of time before I saw my father again.

Chapter 5

Prior

I FROWNED AT ALL OF THE FOOD I'D BOUGHT FOR THE day and wondered if I had too much of it.

"Hey, are the eggs ready for the best part of the meal? The deviled eggs?" Nate asked from my side.

I looked over at him and realized that no, I hadn't made *enough* food.

When we were younger, the Brady brothers had eaten everything in sight. I had no idea how my parents were able to keep a roof over our heads given how much food we consumed. Arden hadn't eaten as much, and not only because she was a girl, because she had been sick—and we hadn't figured it out until it was almost too late.

And that was enough of that train of thought.

"Yes, only I haven't finished making them yet," I said, my hands on my hips as I stared at the vast array of food I had set out on the counter. "As in, I boiled the eggs, but that's about it."

"At least we have a plan," Nate said, and then I was stuffing things back into the fridge while Nate took other things out, and we continued cooking.

"I'm glad that you decided to have us over today instead of us waiting for Arden and Liam to get back into the country."

"They're on a book tour, and Arden likes to be the one to organize these things. I don't mind stepping up, though."

"You're right. And then Cross is the one who does after. We don't contribute much, do we?" Nate asked, winking.

I rolled my eyes. "I've been working hard over a stove for hours, don't even."

"So when are the rest of them getting here?" Nate asked, his focus on filling the eggs.

"Soonish. I know Hazel invited the rest of the girls. And Dakota will probably bring her son."

I hadn't seen Paris since whatever had happened to her that night outside the Mediterranean place. After I got her home, I'd made sure that she had water as she sat on her couch. Then, she'd pretty much forced me out. I'd called Hazel, and she'd said that she and the girls would take care of it. I didn't know what any of that meant, though.

All I knew was that Paris had been hurting. She'd looked as if she had been shocked, leveled a blow that she hadn't been expecting.

And it wasn't any of my business.

I hated to see her in pain like that, but there was nothing I could do.

She was going to be at my house soon, so I would have to think about exactly how to deal with the fact that something was wrong, and I couldn't fix it.

"Is Allison coming, too?" Nate asked, his voice deceptively casual.

I raised a brow. "Yes, she should be on her way soon. Is that a problem?" I asked.

"No, not at all. She just doesn't hang out with us much. Or like...ever. And I don't even think she's met all the girls."

"You need to stop calling them *the girls*," I said.

"True. They call us the boys though, because calling

us the Brady brothers got a little weird after a while," Nate said.

"True." I paused. "I don't even want to call them the ladies. And saying 'Hazel's friends' sounds rude because they're our friends, too. And I don't want to say pact sisters because that sounds really weird."

"We'll just ask them what they want to be called. And you kind of sidestepped the rest of that statement."

I shook my head. "Allison's met Paris."

"She has?"

"You know, at the bar."

Nate raised his brows. "Oh, right. I remember. And Allison got all pissy about it."

I sighed. "We talked about it. We're fine. Don't freak out. Okay?"

"I'm not freaking out. I only want you to be careful. You and Allison seem to have a good thing going, even though it's taking you guys forever to make any headway into being serious."

"You should look in the mirror."

"What? Just because I don't want a serious relationship doesn't mean you shouldn't have one. And you've been with her for what, six months now? I assumed you guys had already been talking about marriage."

I held back a shudder and wondered what the hell that was about.

"Not everyone has to work as fast as Arden and Cross." Our siblings had fallen in love quite quickly with their prospective partners. I wasn't going to fall into that trap. Not that I thought love was a trap, but I was going to take my time. I liked to date. I liked figuring out what I wanted. And I liked the fact that Allison and I were still figuring that out and thinking about it.

Great. Now I was worrying because of Nate. No, if I was honest with myself, it wasn't only Nate. But I honestly didn't want to be too honest with myself right then. As if we had conjured her by just talking about her, my phone buzzed. I looked down at the readout.

"Hey there, my lovely," I said, and Nate rolled his eyes before going back to helping me set up our dinner.

"Hey, I have some bad news."

I wasn't surprised. Allison rarely came to family meals, and I didn't know how to take that. She didn't have any siblings, so she didn't get the whole hanging-out-as-a-group thing. I got that in a way, but this was the fourth time she had canceled in a row. I didn't know how to feel about that.

"Oh?"

"Don't get that tone with me."

"I didn't know I was getting any kind of tone with you, Allison." I started to leave the room when Nate glared at me. I flipped him off, and he grinned before leaving the room.

I took a breath. "I didn't have a tone, Allison."

"I have to work."

"Now?"

"You know, not all of us have a beautiful nine-to-five job."

I was not going to touch that with a ten-foot pole. I didn't want to fight, mainly because the others would be here at any minute, but also, frankly, I was too tired for this crap.

"I'm sorry," Alison said after a moment. "I'll make it up to you," she purred.

I held back a sigh because while the sex between us was great, nothing else seemed to be good. Maybe I was overthinking things, or perhaps everybody telling me I should be in a serious relationship by now was seeping into the rest of my thoughts. I let out a sigh and tried to figure out exactly what I was thinking.

"It's fine. Get back to work. You can come to the next one. It might not be at my house, though. It might be at one of my brother's or my sister's. Is that okay?"

She was silent for a moment, and I wondered what the hell was going on.

"Of course. I can't wait to see you again. Have fun." And then she hung up before I could even say anything.

"You want to tell me what that was about?" Nate asked when he came back into the room, and I shook my head.

"Allison's not coming."

"Figured that. You guys okay?"

"Don't know about that either," I said honestly. "And I don't have time to get into a deep psychological conversation about my relationship with Allison. People are going to be here any minute, and I need to check on the grill."

"The pork's on the smoker, right?" Nate asked, practically licking his lips.

"What do you take me for? I know how to barbecue."

"Famous last words," Nate said with a laugh, and I shook my head and went back out to my deck so I could work on turning some of the meat.

The smell went straight to my gut, and I growled, my mouth watering. I could not wait to dig in. We were going full-on barbecue with ribs, pulled pork, and grilled chicken. Whatever we didn't eat, we'd have for leftovers for the next week. Plus, everyone was going to bring sides and desserts and whatever else they wanted. I wasn't a huge fan of potlucks, but when it came to my family, I trusted them.

Mostly.

I walked back into the house and tilted my head at Cross as he walked into the house.

"Smells amazing," Cross said, his hands full. Hazel was by his side, her hands full, as well. I laughed.

"I made way too much food already, and you guys are seriously packing. What did you guys bring?" I asked, licking my lips.

"I made this bean dip thing that I think you're going to like, and brought some chips. I don't know how to make chips, but I bet Dakota does."

"True. Though I could probably eat that whole bag of chips on my own."

"We brought four bags," Cross said, and I snorted.

"Okay, then. Good to know."

"We also brought fixings for a salad," Cross said. He sighed. "I don't know when we started letting salads into our barbecue, but that's what happens when I bring women."

"You're fortunate that your hands are full because I would hit you right now," Hazel said with a laugh.

"Sorry, babe." He leaned down and kissed her hard on the mouth, and I just shook my head and took everything from Hazel's hands.

"Arden likes salads, too. It's like Cross forgets we grew up with a little sister."

"Believe me, no one can ever forget Arden, but we never used to have salads this big."

"Well, now that I know we have salad, I guess somebody will have to eat these vegetables," Dakota said from the door, her son Joshua at her side.

"Not vegetables," Joshua pouted, his hands full.

"Yes, vegetables. However, we brought dessert, too," Dakota said, and I pumped my fists in the air.

"Yes, now that's what I'm talking about."

"You're going to have to eat your vegetables, too," she said, going up on her tiptoes to kiss me on the cheek. I grinned, fist-bumped Joshua, and then took some of the trays from her hand.

"How much food did you bring?" I asked, straining a bit from the load. The woman was *strong*.

"There're four of you, four of us, plus Joshua here is going through a growth spurt."

"I'm getting big," Joshua said, puffing out his chest a bit.

Nate reached out and took the plate from Joshua's hand so the boy could flex a bit, and we all grinned, making sure that he knew that yes, he was getting big.

"Nice muscles, big man," I said appreciatively.

"Thanks. Macon taught me how to do pull-ups on the bar at the park."

My gaze met my brother's as we both turned to see Macon standing behind them, his hands full of bakery trays, as well.

"I was at the park jogging, saw them, figured I could teach the kid a thing or two about pull-ups."

"I would've gotten to it eventually," Dakota said through gritted teeth.

Well, that was interesting.

"Come on in, let's bring everything in and see what we have."

"Are we late?" Myra asked, her arms full of a case—an actual *case*—of wine. Paris was behind her, two big trays in her hands. "I have yummy little canape appetizers, but Myra has the important stuff. Let her through. She has the wine!"

Everyone laughed and helped each other, and then soon, the food was out, with the doors open so people could easily move from the kitchen and staging area to the outdoor deck that I had built a couple of years ago. Even with all the space available, we had way too much fucking food.

"We're never going to even come close to finishing all of this," I said with a laugh, my arm around Hazel's shoulders. She hugged me tightly before pulling away so she could reach out for a little canape.

"I don't know. Look at the way Nate and Joshua and Macon are diving into my bean dip."

"I thought that's the seven-layer dip," I said, narrowing my eyes at it.

"There are actually nine layers, and Cross called it a bean dip, so that's now what we're calling it."

"I don't know. I'm going to have to dig into it as soon as I get to this pork."

"Don't burn it," Macon growled, taking a bite of salad. He seemed to have an enormous amount of greens on his plate, and since Joshua was looking at him with keen interest, Prior figured out exactly why his brother suddenly liked salad. Because everything that he put on his plate, Joshua did the same.

And I wasn't the only one who noticed.

No, Dakota noticed, too. And from the look on her face, I didn't think she was all that happy about it.

I needed to keep an eye on that, but then again, it wasn't any of my business.

"Looks great," Paris said, coming up to my side as I opened the smoker. She waved smoke from her face and grinned. "Smells amazing. If it wasn't so hot, I might jump in there and snuggle it."

"That's an interesting visual," I said with a laugh. I was doing my best to not look at her. To study her face to see if she was okay. She was acting like everything was normal.

I didn't think *anything* was quite normal.

"Thank you, by the way," she said as I pulled the pork off the smoker.

"For what?" I asked, trying not to drop the damn meat. My brothers would never let me live it down if I did.

"Thank you for that night. Well, for most things recently. But thank you for getting me home. I'm okay now. I just needed to talk with the girls and get it out of my system."

"I'm here if you want to talk to me, too," I said, trying to sound casual. Because I wanted to know what was up. I wanted to help her make things better. However, it wasn't my place.

"Everything will be fine. Just fine." She was talking fast, and I raised a brow.

"It will. I promise. I just needed to get my bearings. And maybe I still do when it comes to certain things. In the end, there's nothing for you to do. The fact that you were there when I needed you...and your brothers, as well? Thank you. There's not much else I can say about that, other than I appreciate it. And I don't want to talk about it ever again."

"Noted. Now, let's dig in."

"It's about time," Nate said, then hugged Paris tightly before getting a plate for himself.

I watched the way Paris leaned into my brother as if she didn't have a care in the world, and nothing was weird between them.

And then I kind of wondered why I was jealous of that? I shouldn't be. After all, she was my friend. My coworker. I shouldn't be insecure about the fact that Paris and I sometimes yelled at each other, or things got awkward between us.

And then my gaze moved across the table to Myra, who stood there with her knuckles white where she gripped the edge. She seemed to see me watching her, and she smiled, her hands relaxing. And then it was as if nothing had happened. As if I hadn't seen anything.

Ever since Cross had brought Hazel home, the dynamics in our family had shifted. I didn't mind it. I liked the new people, the fact that we had grown. Things were very complicated, far more than they used to be.

And I couldn't help but wonder what I was doing with a woman who didn't want to be here. Who wanted nothing to do with what I had with my family.

"You look serious," Joshua said from my side. I looked down at the kid and shook my head.

"Just thinking thoughts. Don't worry. I'm about to dig into my meal."

"Make sure you get salad, though. Because Macon got salad, so that means you should probably get it, too."

I grinned, noticed the way Dakota's brows rose, and piled my plate with salad.

"That sounds like a good idea. Though I'm going to

have to eat some more salad if I'm going to keep up with you. I mean, vegetables do help a boy grow."

"That's what Macon said. And one day, when I'm older, he's going to help me lift weights. He said that he can't lift weights that much right now because he's still getting better from the bad man."

Everybody was quiet for a minute before Hazel cleared her throat.

"You know, I should probably start lifting weights, too," she said with a laugh.

"I like you the way you are," Cross drawled.

"Yes, but I feel like the only thing I lift is a bottle of wine. That probably means I should get something more into my workout regimen."

Everybody started talking about yoga and jogging, and nobody mentioned the bad man or the fact that Macon had even mentioned it to Joshua.

When my brothers got shot, everything changed. I was the one who usually joked around, while Nate joined in. Macon had always been quiet, yet not sullen. Now, something was different about him. Something we couldn't change.

Cross had been shot in the attack as well, but he had Hazel to lean on. Had all of us. Macon had withdrawn, closed in on himself.

And there was nothing I could do about it.

By the time we finished our first course, because I had a feeling we'd go back to it, I was full, happy, and excited to get to the next phase of our gathering.

"Okay, let's wrap everything up so we don't add bacteria to our day. Then, it's football time."

"Wait, we have to play football?" Myra asked, looking down at her open-toed shoes.

"No one actually said football with the invite," Paris said, wincing. "I would have brought tennis shoes."

"Shit, sorry," I said. "We usually play a game when we're together."

"Next time, I'll bring the right shoes," Paris said, and Myra nodded.

"We have the right shoes," Hazel said, hip-bumping Dakota. "Cross warned me because he loves me."

"It was just a happy accident on my part," Dakota said.

"Traitor," Paris said with a laugh.

"Okay, let's get everything cleaned up, then we'll play for a bit. And then figure out something to do with the two barefoot women."

"If you say we should be cheerleaders, I will have to hit you," Paris said, grinning.

An image of Paris in a cheerleading uniform right alongside Myra flashed through my mind, and I purposely pushed it away. No, thank you. I was not going to think about that at all. That was wrong.

And...fuck, I had a girlfriend. A girlfriend I wasn't sure I even liked anymore, but still, I was not an asshole.

We cleaned everything up, dug into more pulled pork and a rib or two because we couldn't help ourselves, and then we slowly made our way out to my back yard.

By the time we were done with the afternoon, we were covered in dirt, had a few bruises, Joshua was asleep on the bench outside after laughing and playing so hard that even I was exhausted watching him, and I just knew that this family was pretty cool. Somehow, we had all come together in this weird mesh of families and connections.

And I didn't think it would be the same if Hazel's friends hadn't shown up.

I met Paris's gaze, and she grinned, but I saw the sadness in her eyes. Once again, I wanted to know if there was something I could do. There was nothing.

As my phone buzzed, and I looked down to see a very not family-friendly photo of Allison on it, I groaned.

And not one of pleasure. Nope. I hadn't expected to see my girlfriend's tits on my phone like that.

Apparently, she was done with work, and still hadn't come here. Instead, she wanted me to go to her house.

That wasn't going to happen tonight, not with my

other plans. I just had to wonder what exactly was going on between us. Our plans weren't meshing. Our paths weren't crossing.

I needed to figure out exactly what the fuck I was going to do about that.

Chapter 6

Paris

HANDS WRAPPED AROUND MY NECK, AND I CLAWED AT the flesh, trying to break free so I could breathe. So that I could live.

The grip merely tightened.

Spots appeared before my eyes.

Screams echoed in my ears.

I struggled, tried to breathe, fought to do something, but the hands wouldn't let go.

And then there were smaller hands on my face, on my shoulders, telling me everything would be okay, leaning close and telling me it would end soon.

"I love you, Paris."

A child's voice, one with a little softness weaved

through it. It filled my ears, and tears streamed down my face as I kicked and thrashed.

I sat up quickly, my eyes open, the dream gone but not that far away. Never far away.

I couldn't seem to catch my breath. I reached up to touch my throat and noticed the blood under my fingernails. The evidence that my nightmare wasn't merely a dream. The blood on my hand was real. I'd scratched myself in my sleep again, and I cursed under my breath before rolling out of bed, my legs shaking, my knees giving way. I clutched at the nightstand and staggered toward the bathroom. I went to the sink, looking at myself in the mirror.

My eyes were wide, my hair standing up in all directions, and I panted. My lips parted as I tried to slow down my breathing and calm my heart rate.

I had a single scratch on my neck, one from my own hands, as I tried to stave off my dream attacker.

I quickly washed the scratch before I brushed my teeth and got into the shower. I put the water as hot as it could go, scalding myself as I tried to wake up, attempted to burn off any excess dream remnants.

The water slid down my back, and I pressed my palms flat against the tile, trying to focus. Attempting to breathe.

I hadn't had that particular dream in a while, and I never wanted to have it again.

I had known it would come. As soon as I'd heard the detective's voice in my ear, I had known that I would have to face these dreams—and possibly face reality.

Because the past had wrapped around me and hadn't let me go quite as much as I'd thought it had.

My father was out of prison. The man who had helped to kill my sister. The asshole who had wrapped his arms around me and pretended to be kind and loving but had really been evil and treacherous.

Everyone who'd had a hand in killing my sister was no longer incarcerated. And they could be at my house at any moment. I hid from them. I had done what I could to make it so I was safe, but was I ever truly safe?

I didn't know.

I didn't know if there would ever be real safety for me.

"Get over it, Paris," I whispered to myself before I pulled away from the wall and washed my hair and my body. I shaved my legs, rinsed off, and got ready for the day.

There was nothing I could do right now when it came to my past. I was as safe as I could be for the moment, even with my father out of prison. I needed to focus on what I could do, rather than the panic of the unknown and what uncertainties could slide through my fingertips at any moment.

I blow-dried my hair and then turned on music, pretending that I could dance away the fear and nightmares.

As I pulled my now-dry hair back into a clip so I could straighten it, I tilted up my chin and pulled out the concealer, dabbing it over the scratch mark. Probably not the best way to deal with things, but I didn't want to field any questions about why I had scratch marks on my neck.

I had been the one to hurt myself this time. There had been no one else. The dreams that haunted me didn't make flesh and blood from nothing, however. The idea of what had once been was something I needed to remember, even if I didn't want to.

While my straightener heated, I finished the rest of my makeup, putting it on like armor. Not only to hide what I dreamed of from others, what I feared, but also to shield part of myself.

Nobody at work needed to know that I had any weaknesses. Some already saw me as weak because of who I was. Perhaps not all, and as an image of Prior filled my mind, I knew it wasn't everybody. People like Benji were why I had to hide part of myself. I was the Shark because I thought they needed me to be. They called me those names because I had to be fierce in the image I projected.

And I lived with that.

I had to be okay with that.

I would work, I would pretend that my makeup and my hair being perfectly done wasn't a symbol of what people needed me to be.

That it wasn't a mask to hide behind, to conceal my dreams and my fears.

I chose my clothing with care, another type of armor, and ignored the fact that my hands shook.

This would mean nothing. It was only a blip.

I could go on living my life as I had before. Trying to find love when I had already decided I wouldn't date. Ignoring a burning attraction to a man I should not want in the slightest and pretending that I wasn't scared to death of everything.

Pretending that the people I worked with didn't hate me or think *I* thought I was too good for them. Because that wasn't it, even in the slightest. That couldn't be farther from the truth.

Nothing I said would change things, so I rolled my shoulders back and told myself I didn't need anybody.

Even if that was the biggest lie of all.

By the time I got to work, I had spread the lies so firmly over my body that I felt as if nobody could see under the layers. And that was fine with me. They didn't need to know everything.

I went to my desk, keeping my office door open because I didn't want those who glared at me—mostly

Benji if I was honest—to think that I thought I was too good for them by hiding myself away. I'd heard someone mumble that before when I just needed some time to focus on my work, so now an open-door concept was how I needed to get things done.

I hated that I cared about what other people thought of me, but that wasn't going to change anytime soon. If I wanted to do the best job possible, I needed people to be able to come to me if they had issues. Hiding from them wasn't going to help my situation.

And if I focused enough on work, I wouldn't worry about the fact that my father was out of prison and could be here at any moment.

It didn't matter that I had a restraining order against him. In the end, it was only a piece of paper that other people would have to enforce. And it wasn't as if, after all this time, somebody would sit there and watch me and ensure that I was okay. I couldn't have security on me at all times—or at any time, for that matter.

So, I would just have to get over it and live my life without fear.

Or at least become better at trying.

"Because that makes complete sense," I whispered to myself.

I sighed and then threw myself into my work, the project I was working on with Prior, something that made me happy. I liked Prior's work. He was diligent, thorough, and always asked the right questions. Yes, there were bugs every once in a while, but finding them was my job, and he never complained when I reported them and opened defect reports. Sometimes, he'd get a little frustrated, but that meant I needed to be more specific in my questions and instructions for how to recreate the problem so he could find the spot in the code that needed to be tweaked.

The fact that both of us could be so open about what we were doing was surprising.

If I were honest with myself, I knew I had judged him from the first moment I saw him. And the second, and probably the third.

I had judged him because of the way he acted with his brothers as if he were carefree. Only I knew that wasn't the case. He reminded me of people at my job, of the man whose place Prior had taken. But that was all on me, not him.

I was getting over it, slowly but surely.

However, others weren't.

"Are you serious about this?" Benji asked, slamming the door behind him.

My pictures rattled on my walls, and I looked up at him, my face stony, my jaw set. My icy armor was the only way to get through to him, or at least make it through my day.

"Hello, Benji. How are you today?"

"Don't give me that."

"You're going to want to watch your tone. Because I *will* report you to HR."

"You keep holding that over my head, and yet you do nothing. I want to know why you keep picking on this assignment. If you don't think I'm good enough, then go to the bosses. You haven't, have you? No. All you do is needle and nitpick, and yet look where you are. You're still only the double-checker. Not a person with the brains to actually get shit done."

On the last word, he slammed out of the room, and I sat there, wondering if he'd have let me speak at all.

Most everybody was already at lunch, something I hadn't noticed because I had been working. I knew Benji had done it for that reason, on purpose.

Not a single soul had been on our floor to hear him talk to me like that.

I could go and complain, and maybe something would be done about it, but I knew Benji was good friends with our boss. They had known each other since they were kids, golfed together twice a week, and drank together three nights out of five.

They were the good old boys, and I was the one left in the dark.

"I'm fine," I whispered.

However, being in the dark had been the wrong phrase to think, because now all I could think about was the dark, and the last time I had been there. With his hands on my throat and the little girl screaming, who wasn't me.

And then there had been no more screaming, no more shouts, nothing. There had been silence: just a cold shadow and an icy void.

"Paris?" Prior asked from the doorway, a bag in his hands, and a frown on his face. "I picked you up a burrito bowl because I saw you hadn't gone for lunch. I can come back." He paused, studying my face. "What's wrong?"

I shook myself out of my memories, knowing they weren't important at the moment. They had never been because I couldn't relive them every day and survive.

I could only remember the good times. And I kept telling myself that, even though the good memories rarely came when I was sleeping.

"A burrito bowl?" I asked, ignoring his other questions.

"Yes. Hopefully, it's what you like. I tried to remember everything you usually get. Though I'm generally so focused on how much extra guac I want on the side, that I sometimes forget." He winked, but I knew he was studying my face, trying to see what was wrong with me.

"Thank you," I said.

Prior didn't need to know everything. I didn't want him to know everything. I didn't want anyone to.

The girls now knew that my father was out of prison, but they didn't know every detail of what my childhood entailed. They didn't know every single little scrape and hit and torture method I had been through—the same as my baby sister.

They didn't ever need to know those things.

They knew I was scared that I had gone into some kind of shock, and that I had been with Prior when I heard the news about my dad. They were the only ones who needed to know. Perhaps Cross knew now because people who loved each other told secrets like that. I understood. As long as I didn't see the pity on his face.

The same emotion I had seen in Prior's gaze for a moment before he blinked it away in the car. Before he did his best to care for me, even though I didn't know how to deal with him.

I wasn't going to tell Prior anything because I didn't want to see that pity again.

"Paris? What's wrong?"

I sat up straighter in my chair and shook my head. And then I began. "Nothing's wrong. I was working and forgot lunch, and now I'm starving. Want to eat in the break room?"

"If you want. Or you can eat in my office. Or we can eat here. Or maybe outside on the balcony. There are a few tables out there."

"I don't know. I mean, I think I accidentally invited you to lunch when you were just dropping mine off."

Prior snorted. "I bought extra lunch because I noticed you hadn't left for your break. We can eat together or separately. It doesn't matter." Prior frowned. "I mean, it does matter because you're my friend, but it doesn't matter in terms of you deciding what you want to do. No pressure."

I let out a sigh and pretended that everything he'd said made sense.

"How about you tell me what I owe you."

He looked defeated for a moment. "How about you just buy me a burrito later?"

"With extra guac?" I asked him, and he smiled.

His eyes brightened, and some of the tension he had been holding in his shoulders seemed to slide away.

Tension about my reaction? Or something else?

And why did I want to know? Why did I want to ask?

"You know, I should get back to work. It's been a slow day for me, and I could use the focus. Thank you for the burrito bowl. I'll get yours next time."

He handed over my lunch, studying my face. I did my best to blank any emotions other than peace. As I said, he didn't need to know anything was wrong with me.

Even though that was far from the case.

I went back to work, having devoured my burrito bowl quickly, annoyed, and a little surprised that Prior had figured out exactly what I liked.

The fact that I could likely tell him what he wanted on his burrito told me we probably had been working together for too long, even over the relatively short time period he'd been in my department.

By the end of the workday, my shoulders hurt, my lower back ached, and I knew I was going to have a stress headache later. I had gotten tons of work done, but between Benji's attitude and my nightmare, I'd felt like I was on the verge of throwing up or screaming for most of the day.

I packed up my things and headed out towards the elevator to go home.

Prior was already there, waiting for the lift. He smiled. "Look at us, on the same schedule again."

"Apparently."

"You don't need to sound so excited about that."

"Sorry, it's been a long day."

"Seems like. I got here a little bit before you because I had a couple of things to finish up, but we're still the last people here."

I looked around, my eyes wide. "I didn't even notice that. What is wrong with me?" I could have slapped myself for that thought because first, I did not want to think about what was wrong with me, and second, I didn't want him to question it.

"Probably because we're both in the middle of a tough project. I get it, sometimes things just flow, and you forget about everything else. Which kind of sucks because I'm already late to meet Allison."

"Late again?" I asked, wondering why I felt a little clutch in my belly at the mention of her name. What was wrong with me? I was a horrible person. Completely horrible.

"We have to talk," he said, an emotion in his voice that I couldn't quite name.

"Like *the* talk? Or a talk?" I asked as we got into the elevator. There was an awkward silence then, even more awkward than a typical elevator ride, and I winced. "Never mind. You don't have to tell me anything."

"No. I'm just figuring out exactly what the talk is going to be. I don't think it's going to work out between Allison and me, and I hate that. Because I feel like I failed."

Emotions swamped me, and I couldn't quite figure out what they were. Sadness? Pity? Jealousy? No, it couldn't be the latter. I didn't even know him and Allison and their relationship enough to feel too sad or jealous about it. I was probably mixing up everything going on within me and couldn't focus on what he was saying.

"I'm sorry."

"Me, too. You know I'm good at a lot of things. But, apparently, relationships are not one of them."

"You're talking to the woman who has had six horrible bad blind dates after years of trying to do it on my own. At least you had a decent run of it."

Prior winced. "I'm glad our scorecards look the way they do. I think Cross and Hazel are the only two that succeeded at any of this."

"Probably. We're not going to tell the two of them that because they're already going to have big heads as it is."

"Preach." He smiled, shook his head, and headed towards his car. "I'll see you on Monday?"

"Sounds like a plan. Have fun with the boys this weekend." I paused. "And I'm sorry about Allison."

He gave me a look, his eyes sad. "Me, too. Be safe."

Then he turned the corner, headed to where his car was parked, and I made my way to mine.

I let out a breath, wondering what I was going to do this weekend. Organize my spice rack? Maybe go shoe shopping. Or perhaps start that new thirty-day yoga plan that I had been putting off for about eighty-seven days.

I had just reached my car when something smashed

down on the back of my head. It took me a moment to realize what had happened, but in the next instant, I was on the ground, my hands digging into the asphalt, and a shocked scream echoing from my mouth.

"Bitch!"

Then someone kicked me in the ribs and stomped on my foot. There was a slap and a kick, and I couldn't tell from which direction they came. Everything was spinning, and I rolled on my back, trying to fight off whoever was there, but I couldn't.

I couldn't see.

There was something over the attacker's face, but then I saw double, and I couldn't tell up from down anymore.

Then I couldn't do anything.

"Paris?" someone yelled, and then I heard the sound of shoes on pavement as someone ran towards me. The shadow above me cursed, and I couldn't even tell if it was a man or a woman.

I was so dizzy. I wanted to sleep.

And then I rolled over and tried to crawl away. I had to do something.

Someone was calling me, reaching for me, and I cringed. I wanted to go home. Wanted this to end.

I couldn't do anything. I couldn't think, couldn't breathe. Something was wrong. Something was terribly wrong.

As I dug my fingers into the pavement, my fingertips bloody, and my lungs burning, a strange thought entered my mind.

I had started my day waking from a dream of death, pain, and screams, unable to breathe.

And now I would end it the same, only in real life.

Chapter 7

Prior

BILE COATED MY TONGUE. I TRIED TO SWALLOW IT down, but I couldn't. There was nothing I could do. I sat in the waiting room, my hands shaking as I looked down at them, trying to figure out what the fuck was going on.

Paris was hurt. Damn hurt. And there was nothing I could do about it. I wasn't even sure there was anything I *could* do. I'd gotten the ambulance to her. I'd tried to see who had hurt her, but I hadn't been able to *do* anything. If I had left Paris to go chase after who had hurt her, she would have been there alone, bleeding and in pain.

I couldn't have done that.

Instead, I called 911 and prayed. And now I was sitting in the waiting room of the hospital, trying to figure out exactly what had happened. The cops had already come and gone, though I knew they would be talking to me again. After all, Paris had been hurt, and I was the only witness. And probably a suspect at this point, I didn't know, but my mind kept going in a thousand different directions.

So, here we were. Me trying to figure out what the fuck I was going to do and waiting to hear from the doctors. Even though I wasn't sure they were going to let me know what was going on with her because I wasn't family or her emergency contact.

As if I had conjured her, Hazel flew into the waiting room, Cross right behind her.

"Have they said anything?" Hazel asked, her face pale, and her eyes wide. There was a determined set to her face, and I was grateful for that. She would be able to get answers since she was one of Paris's emergency contacts. Paris didn't have any family, so she had put her group of friends on her list.

Did I even have my entire family on my list? Or just Cross? After Cross and Macon had been shot, I'd told myself I'd make sure that all of my affairs and contacts were in order, but I wasn't even sure I'd done that.

I was on Arden's list considering that my little sister was constantly in and out of the hospital thanks to lupus. The others? I didn't know.

"Hey, snap out of it."

I blinked up at Cross, who glared down at me, even though there was still worry on his face.

"You went off in a different direction mentally. Answer the question. Any word?"

I shook my head. "No, and I probably wouldn't hear anything anyway. You guys needed to be here. Or at least Hazel."

Cross gave me a tight nod, understanding flickering across his face.

Hazel was the one who spoke. "Because you're not family, or on whatever list they have. Okay. I'm going to go see what I can find out." She hurried off, and Cross stood in front of her, his gaze burning holes into me.

"Do you want to tell me what happened?" he asked, and I swallowed hard, then looked up at my big brother.

"We were getting off work, heading to our cars. I went one way, and she went the other since we didn't park on the same side of the building. Then I heard a scuffle or something, and her scream, and I ran towards her. But I was too late. I didn't see who it was, just someone wearing all black and a hat, which doesn't help at all."

"You got her here. That's all that matters for now," Cross said, and I shook my head.

"It doesn't feel like it. It feels like I should have been

there. Should've waited until she got into her car and drove off. Instead, I left her alone."

"You had no reason to think she was going to get attacked in your parking lot. You can't blame yourself for this."

"Can't I? I said I'd make sure she was safe."

"You're doing that now."

Cross paused, and I looked up at him. "What?"

"You think it was that guy at work that pisses you off?" he asked, and I blinked. The idea hadn't even occurred to me. I'd had my head so far up my ass that I hadn't gotten past my own guilt to think who could have done this.

"I don't know. Maybe. Maybe not. Hell. I don't think Benji would get violent. Jesus. I didn't even tell the cops that he and Paris had an issue. I will. I'll tell them right now. She would. Right?"

"Unless she doesn't want to make waves at work."

"Fuck. You're right. She hates being seen as weak. Feels like she can't be anything but strong, and with some of the people that work there, I can see that actually being an issue."

Cross stared at me for a minute, and I blinked.

"What?" I asked.

"You seem to be spending a lot of time with Paris these days."

I flipped him off, ignoring a gasping sound from the woman next to us.

"Here? *This* is where you're going to have that talk with me?"

"Sorry." Cross closed his eyes and let out a breath. "It's just bringing up memories again. You know?"

"At first, I thought the only memories that would come back for us was every time we saw Arden in a hospital bed all hooked up to a bunch of machines and in pain. Now, it's you and Macon. And even Hazel."

"You didn't see Hazel on the ground, bloody, and left tied up. I never want to see that again, not even in my dreams. And yet, here we are, with another of us hurt."

"Doesn't make any sense to me," I said, frowning.

"What doesn't make any sense to you?" Cross asked.

"That this keeps happening. I know we've lived in a decently safe bubble, even with the issues we had before. I still can't believe that she's hurt like this. And there's fucking nothing we can do about it."

"She made it this far because you were there to help her."

"Maybe. But if I had only been a second faster, or if I hadn't let her go off on her own, we wouldn't be here at all."

"I'm going to tell you something that you've told me before."

"And what is that?" I asked, nervous.

"If you spend the rest of your life on what-ifs, you're going to hurt yourself and those you love in the end. So, focus on what you can do. And while we're figuring that out, we can wait and see how Paris is doing. Because she's going to be okay, right? There's no other option."

I nodded at Cross's words, knowing that he was right. And I *had* said something similar to him when we were all worried about each other. So, I would wait. And I would hope to hell that Paris was going to be okay. She was my friend. My coworker. Nothing more than that. But hell, I just wanted her to be okay.

"She's going to be all right," I said softly.

"Yes, she will."

Cross took the seat on the other side of me, and we sat there, waiting until Dakota came in with her son, and Myra walked through the double doors, searching for us. When their gazes finally landed on us, their eyes narrowed, relief crossing their features a bit as they came towards us.

"Any news?" Myra asked, her voice crisp.

"Still waiting for Hazel to come back out."

I looked over at Cross, frowning. "She should be out soon, shouldn't she?" I asked.

"I'm here," Hazel said, and I stood up so quickly that I almost knocked Joshua over. I put my hand on his shoulder, steadying him before letting go. He slid his hand into mine and his other into his mom's.

I gave it a squeeze and looked down at the kid.

"She'll be okay, right?" Joshua asked.

"Yes, she will," Hazel answered for all of us, and my shoulders sagged. I leaned against the chair slightly. I gave Joshua's hand another squeeze, and he did the same back before letting go and holding his mom around the waist.

The doors opened again, and Macon and Nate were there, practically storming in. The rest of the waiting room stared at us, and I didn't blame them. Especially considering that the Brady brothers were pretty big dudes and we took up a lot of space. Now, there was a whole group of us waiting. I only needed to know if Paris was going to be okay.

"She's going to be fine," Hazel repeated. "She needs a little bit of time to get some medicine and rest. She'll be going home soon."

Dakota smiled and opened her mouth to say something, but Macon spoke first.

"Hey, Joshua, now that we know your Aunt Paris is doing fine, let's go check out the vending machines."

Dakota narrowed her eyes. "We don't need to add sugar to this day," she said.

"No, but we can still look," Macon said, holding out his hand.

Joshua took it and smiled at his mom. "I'll be fine. You guys can talk about the adult stuff while Macon takes me away."

I held back a smile because Joshua was way too smart for his own good sometimes.

Macon and Dakota stared at each other—or rather they glared—and I waited to see what would happen.

After what seemed like forever, the standoff ended, and Dakota gave a tight nod before Macon and Joshua turned and exited the waiting room to presumably head to where the vending machines were located.

"Okay, tell us," I said, my voice shaky. Everyone stared at me for a minute before looking back at Hazel.

"She has a mild concussion, no broken bones, a few scrapes, and one cut that might require stitches. They're still working on that. She's awake, a little groggy, and pissed off."

That put a smile on my face.

"So, a pissed-off Paris seems about right," I said, and the guys gave me a look, while the girls just smiled.

"I'm so glad that you were there," Hazel said before reaching out to hug me. I squeezed her back, kissed the top of her head, and then moved away quickly before Cross could glare at me for touching his woman. Not that he would hurt me, but I didn't want my brother to get any ideas.

"So, she's going home soon?" Nate asked with his hands stuffed into his pockets. He stood by Myra, and the two of them were determinedly *not* looking at each other. I still didn't know what was up between them, but I didn't have time to deal with that right now.

"Probably tomorrow. The staff wants to keep her overnight for observation. You guys can head home. They're not going to let anyone back there right now. And frankly, we all know that she wouldn't want you guys to see her like this anyway."

"You'll keep me updated?" I asked, the urgency in my tone surprising even me.

"Of course, I will," Hazel said, sliding her hand into Cross's.

I swallowed hard, stuffed my hands into my pockets like Nate, and gave a tight nod.

"Sounds good. Tell her...I don't know, just tell her I'm glad she's okay."

Hazel gave me a weird look, and then I smiled and walked away, Nate right behind me. Macon walked back into the waiting room as we were leaving and raised his brows.

"Everything's okay. We're headed home."

"Sounds good. I'll follow you out. Let me just get this guy back to his mom."

"I'm good on my own," Joshua said.

Macon snorted. "Sure you are, kid. Do we honestly want your mom to rip me a new one for letting you walk around by yourself in a place that we don't know?"

"Fine. I am almost an adult now."

That made me smile.

Joshua continued. "You know they're changing the age of a teenager to my age soon."

Macon snorted again, shook his head, and led Joshua back to where his mom was.

I met Nate's gaze, and we both cracked up laughing, shaking our heads.

I was pretty sure I had said something similar to my parents back in the day, and it reminded me that while life moved on, some things stayed the same.

I hated that I had no idea what was going on inside me when it came to Paris. No idea what I would have done if she had been hurt more than she had.

I was still going to fucking blame myself. I should've been faster. Never should have left her. Should've found a way to keep her safe.

And I hadn't.

I wouldn't have forgiven myself if I hadn't run when I did. If I had gotten into my car a second earlier, I might have missed that scream. And she would have been there all alone. And God knows what would've happened.

That bile came back into my throat, and I swallowed

it down, then got into my car, saying goodbye to my brother before heading home.

I didn't want to talk to anybody. I didn't want to focus on anything.

Fuck, I had forgotten somebody important.

I was supposed to meet Allison—and probably break it off.

I hadn't even told her where I was going.

Watching my friend get hurt had pushed all thoughts of everything and everyone else out of my head. Fuck.

I couldn't deal with this.

Allison wasn't mine anymore, and I had to make sure she understood that. I had to figure out how to explain that we had grown in different directions.

And fuck, this was probably why I wasn't good at relationships.

I pulled into my garage, turned off my car, and rubbed my temples.

I just wanted a beer, needed to forget the day and relax, but that wouldn't be happening. I was going to have to call Allison and apologize for standing her up.

And then find a way to break it off because it wasn't fair to either of us to keep this going.

I made my way into my home and frowned when I heard sounds from the back of the house.

Considering that I had just left my brothers, it couldn't be them.

The hairs on the back of my neck rose, and I looked around for a weapon, but then I realized who was back there.

I recognized that purse, those shoes, and even the fucking bra.

And the deep voice that went along with the very familiar feminine voice? No, she wasn't alone. She wasn't waiting for me.

Fuck this.

How the hell had she gotten in?

I slowly made my way to the back of the house, wondering if I should just say screw it and leave and let her have a good time in my bed.

Instead, I made it to my bedroom door, looked at my bed where the woman I was currently dating was riding her ex, a man I had met once or twice. I let out a laugh.

Because why the fuck not?

At my laugh, the man froze, his hands digging deep into her hips, but Allison turned over her shoulder and winked.

"It's about time you got home."

Un-fucking-believable.

"Jesus. You could've just texted. Isn't that what people

do these days? Is there a reason you had to fuck your ex in my bed? *My* bed."

She continued moving, and the guy started shaking as if trying to dislodge her, but Allison did what she wanted.

"What? You weren't getting me off, so I figured I'd do what I had to."

"Seriously? That's the line you're going with? Fine. Get out. It's done. It's over. You already know this. Get out of my fucking house. And give me back the fucking key I didn't know you had."

"I watered your plants. So, I kept the key."

"I don't fucking care. Get out. Now."

She rolled her eyes and then swiveled her hips before getting off.

I turned because there were some things I didn't need to see and ignored the pair as the guy started grumbling low about how he'd thought this was her place.

The guy must be dumber than a bag of rocks if he thought this was her house. But whatever, I didn't have time to worry about that right now. I just needed her out.

The guy mumbled his apologies before running out, his shoes in his hands, and his zipper undone, closing the front door behind him.

I turned to see Allison slowly putting on her earrings, her lips swollen, and her makeup smeared a bit.

"Was it worth it?"

"You tell me. You love her, you're spending all your time with her, and all you did was leave me alone. You deserved this."

What. The. Fuck?

"You know what, fuck you."

"You weren't doing that, and that was the problem. You don't get to talk to me that way."

"You basically broke into my house. You're fucking your ex in my bed, and you have the nerve to say that? Do you want to know where I was? Why don't you fucking ask me, Allison?"

"You were with her, weren't you?"

"I was in the hospital because she got attacked in our work parking lot. I was waiting to make sure that she was alive. Whatever. We already knew this relationship was over, even before now. You just made sure to bang that nail right into the coffin."

"Oh my God," she whispered, her eyes wide.

"Don't act as if you care. Get out. And leave my fucking key."

She opened her mouth to say something, but then she left, her hands shaking. I honestly didn't care.

We hadn't been in a serious or healthy relationship.

I didn't feel guilty, I couldn't. Maybe I would later.

For now, I would call a locksmith and change my

locks, just in case. I wondered what the fuck else I was going to do.

Because I didn't love Paris, not even a little.

Yet I *was* attracted to her. And that was a problem on many fronts.

I had never acted on those feelings, had never done anything untoward.

Allison didn't believe me. Though that didn't matter. Nothing mattered anymore.

Damn, I wanted that fucking beer. And to forget.

I knew I would never be able to get the sound of Paris's scream out of my head. Not until the end of my days.

Never.

Chapter 8

Paris

GRAVEL SCRAPED MY CHIN, MY FACE. I BLINKED, trying to get the cobwebs out of my mind. There was something wrong. I couldn't hear anything, couldn't speak. It was as if I stood in a vacuum, everything was moving too slowly, and yet I wasn't even on my feet. I couldn't make sense of it at all. Nothing made sense.

My cheek hurt, and my hands ached where my palms bled from where the gravel had pierced. My knees burned, as well. And then I was on my back, and someone's hands were around my throat. I clawed, my fingernails digging in but not gaining purchase in the gloves. Why was the person wearing gloves? Had they been prepared for this? Why couldn't I focus? Why couldn't I think?

I kicked and thrashed, but it wasn't enough. It wasn't going to be enough.

I gasped out a name, but not my own, not even a call for help.

Tracey.

Tracey wasn't here.

She was dead.

My baby sister was dead, and I wasn't near the trailer. Instead, I was dying here, begging for someone to help me. And yet nobody could help.

I was little, too young to remember, and yet far too old to forget.

I was wearing the same clothes I'd had on when they killed her, and I was now covered in blood and screaming.

This time, the shadow above me turned into the man or woman who had attacked me.

I knew this had to be a dream. Or maybe a memory.

Perhaps I was mixing them up, but I couldn't focus enough to pull myself out of the nightmare.

I couldn't scream or slap my face or pinch my arms or do anything to pull myself out of the dream.

Nothing worked.

And the hands around my neck clutched harder.

I blinked, and the woman above me had my eyes and my smile, but there was something evil in it.

"Mom."

She didn't answer. She just kept squeezing.

She was killing me. My mother was killing me.

Like she'd helped to kill Tracey.

I blinked again, and it was no longer her.

Now, it was my dad.

And just like my mom, he wasn't the age he should be now. He was the same age he had been when he killed me.

No, not me. My sister. When he killed Tracey.

There was no going back. There was no fixing this.

I was dying, screaming.

Help.

Then, somebody helped me.

"Paris."

"Paris."

My eyes shot open, and I sat up and screamed.

Suddenly, Dakota was there, holding me softly as I cried against her neck, her hands smoothing down my hair and holding me close.

I clung to her as I never had before. I hadn't let anybody hold me like this before.

No, that wasn't the case, was it? I had cried in the others' hold when they were here for me throughout the past week when I woke up and screamed because the nightmares were back. There was no holding them back any longer.

"You're safe. You're here. I've got you."

I pulled away then, needing to suck in gulps of air as I wiped my face.

"I'm sorry."

Dakota looked at me and shook her head. "Stop it. Do not be sorry."

"I hate crying on you. I already cried on everyone else."

Dakota smiled softly, looking more motherly than I had ever seen her before. "The fact that you trust me enough to even cry in my presence means a lot. And you're allowed to feel like this. You're allowed to be scared. Something horrible happened. But you're safe."

"Maybe." I ran my hands over my face a few times and then let out a breath.

"My ribs hurt."

"I'm not surprised. They're bruised. So much so that the doctor thought it might have been better if you had broken one."

I tried to laugh and then held my side as I let out a slow breath. "Great. Breaking me would be better than what I'm feeling right now," I grumbled. "I hate sounding like I'm riding the pity train."

"You're allowed to do that for the next few hours. I'll give you that time. And then, after that, we'll take you off the train and get you into some coping mechanisms. I'm sure between the four of us, we can probably figure those out."

I rolled my eyes and smiled—the first real one I'd had since the attack.

"I still can't believe they have no idea who it was," I said, slowly rolling out of bed. Dakota was there in an instant, helping me up, and I leaned into her, hating that I felt so weak. I had no broken bones, a few stitches, and some very bruised ribs. My concussion was the worst of it, and I was still on concussion protocol, but so far, it looked like I was out of the woods. So much so that I was going back to work on Monday. My boss, the asshole that he was, had griped about having to give me a week off, but my doctor had gone to bat for me. And so had Prior. He didn't know that I knew, but I had heard through the grapevine, namely Hazel, that he had fought for me.

I didn't know what to think about that.

He had fought for me to have time to heal, had physically battled for me, too when I was in the parking lot. He had fought for me. Had probably saved my life.

And I hadn't heard from him at all.

I knew he was giving me space, but it still felt weird. And then it felt weirder that it felt strange, considering that he was nothing to me except for a new friend and a coworker.

His name had been on the card from my company when they sent flowers and a bagel basket with a fantastic spread of cream cheeses. Everybody's name had been on the card except Benji's, and I was happy about that because I didn't even want to look at that man's name in my house.

Other than that, I hadn't heard a word from Prior.

I needed space and time to heal, but I still wanted to thank him.

And I had no idea what I was going to say when it was time to do that. It wasn't like I was good at this whole thing. I hated being in debt to anyone, and I knew I was going to be indebted to Prior for the rest of my life for what he had done.

Because if he hadn't been there...?

No, I didn't want to think about that. Of course, my dreams let me think about that enough. I didn't need to obsess while awake, as well.

"Do you need help in the shower?" Dakota asked, and I looked at her before holding back a laugh.

"That sounds like the start of some very good porn."

"Honey, if it was the start of a porno, I'd already have you in the shower," Dakota said it so deadpan that I burst out laughing, and then groaned as I held my side.

"Stop making me laugh. It hurts, it hurts."

She winced and helped me hobble over to the bathroom.

"I'm sorry. I can't help it if I'm amazing."

I smiled then, looking at the woman who was like a sister to me. Even if that gave me a little pang to think about, it was the truth.

"Thank you."

"Aw, I love you."

"Do you love me enough to take the next place in the pact?" I asked out of the blue. She tripped over her own feet, and thankfully, I was already leaning against the doorway so I didn't get hurt.

"What?"

"What?" I countered.

"Where on earth did that come from?"

"I honestly have no idea. Other than the fact that I told Prior that I was giving up on this whole dating thing. So, we tried, I'm done. Now, it's your turn."

An odd look crossed her features, and she shook her head. "No. As soon as you're up to it, we'll find you a nice date."

"No, we won't. I mean, the last time you found me someone, the man wanted me to join his wife in bed. And while that might've been fun and kinky, it wasn't what I was looking for."

Dakota burst out laughing, and I grinned.

"You would have joined in?"

"I'm still young. Ish. A little banged up, sure, but no... probably not with them. You never know, though." I winked, and she grinned.

"Now that we know that that might be on the table, we should add that to our notes for the next person."

I flipped her off. "No. I want a good date. Not only a fling or a man or woman who's going to take me to bed with five others."

"Five? Wow, a little adventurous, aren't you?"

"Shut up. You know what I mean."

"Maybe not. Now I'm just picturing a sixsome, or is that an orgy at that point? When do we know when it's an orgy? Like how many people have to be involved? And do all these people have to touch for it to be an orgy, or is it a form of -some. Like a threesome or an eightsome?"

"I have no idea, but now I have weird sketch drawings in my head of stick people trying to stick each other."

Dakota wiped tears from her eyes as I smiled, shaking my head.

"You're back up to your normal dorkiness level. Looks like you're feeling better." She was silent for a moment, and I hoped she wasn't going to bring it up.

I wasn't that lucky.

"You called out your sister's name again. Have you talked to your therapist?"

"Over the phone, yes. Myra was in the other room, and she forced me to do it."

Dakota grinned. "Well, Myra has a talent for forcing you to take care of your mental health. And your physical health. She's our friend for a reason."

"She's as pushy as the rest of you, but I love you guys. I don't know what I'm supposed to do. The dreams keep coming, just like the nightmares of what happened in the parking lot. Maybe if they found the guy who did it, it would make things better. But I don't think so. My subconscious is a bitch."

"You said yourself that you're a bitch, so aren't you used to that?" Dakota asked, looking sweet as sin.

"Bitch."

"I'm learning my bitchiness. I'm a mom. I'm usually only bitchy when I'm in mama bear mode."

"Maybe, but I think you hide your bitchiness under all that sweet cream and sugar."

"And that could be why I do not have a date." She held up her hands before I could speak. "And it's not my turn. You may say you're done with dating, but we both know that's not the case. You want happiness. Hazel found hers, and it's our turn. You're up first. And then I guess it's Myra, and then I will take up the charge at the end."

"What did we get ourselves into?" I asked, frowning down at my hands.

"I don't know. I don't think we had any idea what we were getting ourselves into. I thought it would be easy to have fun on a single date. It clearly isn't." Dakota winced. "Not that I'm saying that it's your fault or anything."

"Thanks," I said, sarcasm lacing my tone.

"I'm only saying that dating is hard, and I don't want to go to apps or online dating. I want people to introduce me to happy people who will make me happy. Or, I don't know, someone who likes me for more than my baked goods." She paused. "And baked goods is a euphemism, yet isn't in this case."

I laughed at that. "Good to know. Though I don't think I'll ever be able to eat your baked goods again."

She crossed her eyes, and I laughed.

"Go take a shower. I'll get you something to eat."

"I'm not hungry," I said quickly.

"I don't actually care. You haven't eaten since last night, and you're going to eat now. So get over yourself."

"Is this what you say to Joshua every morning?"

"Sometimes. This morning, he was off to school quickly because he had a school project that he wanted to show off."

She practically said that through her teeth, and I reached out to grip her hand. "What?"

"He had to interview a new and fun person in his life, and he picked Macon."

"What's wrong with Macon?" I asked, honestly curious.

"There's nothing wrong with him, other than the fact that he's not Joshua's father." Some other emotion filled her eyes, but she pushed on quickly before I could say anything. "And I don't know if I like the fact that Joshua's clinging to him as much as he is. Even more so than any of the other Brady brothers. There's just...I don't know, something I don't like. But I'm going to have to deal with it for now because I don't want to break my little boy's heart. However, if Macon does that, I will have to castrate him."

"Ouch," I said, not sure what else to say.

"He'd deserve it. Nobody hurts my son."

"Has he?"

"I don't know him well enough to tell. But I don't think so. And that's what worries me. Anyway, enough about me. Go shower, I'll get you some food, and then we will focus on your next date."

"I already told you, it's your turn. I'm not going on any more."

Dakota ignored me. "Hazel and Myra both have half days today and will be here soon, so you can just get right over yourself and start thinking about what you're looking for on a date for real. Because that is our new brainstorm."

"Dakota."

"Don't *Dakota* me. We can't fix anything else right now, so we're going to fix this. You are friends with three fixers, and you, my friend, are the worst of the bunch. So, go get showered, get all pretty or whatever you want to do because you're always pretty, and I kind of hate that, and then you're going to come out and eat some food, and then we're going to set you up on a wonderful date."

She turned on her heel and stalked out of the bathroom, and I blinked at her, shaking my head.

I did not want to go on a date. Not even a little.

Add in the fact that somebody's face that I shouldn't even be thinking about flashed in my mind at that thought, and it told me I was already headed into dangerous territory.

I gripped the edge of the sink and let out a breath, controlling my pain and my mind, telling myself that it would all be okay.

When I looked at my reflection, for an instant I saw the little girl that had screamed, but then I was back to being me—dorky, sarcastic, and possibly a little bitchy Paris.

I didn't know who I would be if I had grown up in a happy family. If Tracey were alive today.

I would have been able to watch her grow and help her figure out life while I figured out mine. I might have become a completely different person.

I might be happy.

I didn't know where that thought had come from, and I quickly threw it from my mind.

Maybe I kept having to go on these dates as penance. Or perhaps it was because I didn't know what I wanted.

I for sure did not want Prior Brady.

I needed to focus on the future. And that meant maybe another guy or girl, just somebody who made me happy.

Who thought about me and put me first and didn't make me feel like I was doing something wrong.

I wanted a future, I wanted happiness.

While all of this tangled in my mind, I still wasn't sure it could happen if I didn't know who had attacked me. It had crossed my mind a couple of times that it could have been my mother or father.

Detective Buker had been firm that he knew where both of them were during the attack. He had been the one to go after them and check on their alibis.

It hadn't been them. It hadn't been Benji either, even though for an instant, I'd thought it might have been him.

There were no cameras in the parking lot, something that was going to be changed.

And according to Hazel, I had Prior to thank for that, too.

So, I didn't know who had attacked me, and I might not ever know. If it wasn't attached to my past, and it wasn't Benji, then who was it? Maybe one of the dates that I'd been on before? I didn't know. I didn't think so, though.

Maybe whoever it was only wanted my purse.

They hadn't taken that, though. Instead, they had hurt me, bruised me, and gave me nightmares.

I still didn't know who it was or who it could be.

The one name that kept coming to my mind no matter what, was the person who had been there when I needed help.

Prior had been there.

And I didn't know what I was going to do about that.

I would have to face him soon. I needed to thank him and figure out what to say.

And all the while, I'd have to do my best not to think about him in any other way.

He wasn't mine. He was someone else's.

Maybe that was exactly why I needed to go on another date. To put Prior out of my mind. And the nightmares, too.

As I looked at my reflection in the mirror, I didn't think I would be able to forget anytime soon. The bruises would fade, and my ribs would heal, but my nightmares would remain—like always.

No matter how far I looked into the future, my past was always there to haunt me.

Always.

Chapter 9

Prior

"PARIS IS BACK TO WORK TODAY, RIGHT?" NATE ASKED as we turned the corner, the sun coming up in front of us.

I nodded, let out a breath, and panted a bit since we were jogging. I hated talking while I ran. Nate loved the exercise, and since he was the one who wanted to jog this morning, and I needed to clear my head, I had to deal with the chatting. "Yes. I don't think she's working a whole day."

"Your boss is letting that play out?" Nate asked.

"Yes," I said, my chest burning. I was running way too fast, trying to keep up with Nate. It wasn't that I wasn't an okay runner, it was more that Nate was fucking good and could do this for hours. I liked to run a couple of miles and call it a day. Nate could probably run marathons if he tried.

However, he was my baby brother, and I had to at least *try* to keep up with him. It was the principle of the thing.

Nate had always been this way, though. The best athlete of us all. And it didn't escape our notice that while he might be the best athlete, his twin sister was the one who was the sickest of us all, lupus trying to take her from us every time she got ill.

I frowned, pushing those weird thoughts from my mind. I didn't know why I was getting all philosophical when it came to the family. Maybe it was because I was trying not to think about Paris and the fact that I was going to see her today.

I didn't know why it should bother me. I kept thinking about her screaming, and what would've happened if I hadn't been there. What would've happened if I had been two seconds late, or perhaps two seconds early? Would she have been as hurt if I hadn't gotten there on time? Or maybe I should have walked her to her damn car so she wouldn't be hurt at all.

I kept thinking about it, over and over again, but I couldn't push it from my mind, even though I should.

I couldn't fix this. I couldn't help her.

"Prior?"

We turned into my driveway, and I leaned forward, resting my hands on my knees as I tried to catch my breath.

"What?"

"I asked if your boss is okay with Paris working half days. Are you okay?" "Fine. Just out of breath. You're faster than me."

"I've always been faster than you. And I have better endurance. And I'm prettier."

"Whatever you say," I said, flipping him off.

"You're an ass, but because you're a hero, I guess you're allowed to be."

I cringed, hating that word.

"I need water, a shower, and coffee. And don't call me that."

"Why?" Nate asked.

"Because I'm not. Paris still got hurt."

" you were still there for her. Paris is one of us now. Even if she weren't, you would've helped her, any of us would have, but you were there, and you did your thing. You protected her. She's practically family now that Hazel's going to be part of our clan."

"And we always take care of family," I said, walking

into my house and going towards the fridge so I could chug water. I got down two glasses, poured a couple of waters, and chugged the contents while Nate did the same before we went for more.

"You know, we've always had a decently big family with the five of us kids and Mom and Dad, but now with Arden marrying, and Cross being with Hazel, things keep getting bigger." Nate frowned and looked down at his glass.

"What's wrong?"

"Nothing. Just thinking about how some things have changed, and I felt like we weren't really ready for it."

"Why would we need to be ready for our siblings to get married? Mom and Dad have never once pressured us to get married."

"You're right. It's just...I don't know. Ignore me."

"No, I won't. What's wrong?"

"Nothing's wrong. I guess I got a little light-headed from the run."

I let him lie because Nate never got dizzy from his runs, but I poured him more water, and then I leaned against the counter, staring at my baby brother.

Nate was generally loud, like me. Cross and Macon growled more than we did and tended to be a little quieter. Arden was the mediator between the four of us, and we were her protectors. Though in the end, some-times—or most of the time—she protected us, too.

Nate had his secrets. I didn't know what they were, though. He was cagey on occasion, even though I didn't think others noticed. Or maybe they did. Perhaps we were all so good at protecting each other that we let ourselves guard our individual secrets.

If he was hurting, though, he would tell us. And even though I like to needle him because he was my baby brother, I would let him have his secrets. After all, I was keeping my own.

Like the fact that I thought I liked Paris.

Fuck. I shouldn't. Not only was she my coworker and part of the whole crew now, and dating anyone within the group would make things tricky and unmanageable, but it was also just wrong.

Allison had used Paris as her scapegoat to cheat on me and to push me out of the relationship that I was already trying to get out of on my own.

And I didn't like the fact that Allison might've been right. Even in the vaguest sense of the word.

"I need a shower. You showering here?"

"Um, I know that you've been through a lot losing Allison and everything," Nate began. I didn't want to hear the end of that sentence, but I let my little brother go on.

"I don't want to shower with you. Although you could probably get the places on my back that I have trouble reaching, that whole incest thing gets complicated."

"Please, for the love of God, never ever say incest when it has to do with our family again," I said, and Nate laughed.

"Sorry. I started with a joke, and then it got creepy."

"Very, very creepy. I would hit you, but I need the energy to work."

"Need the energy to sit behind a desk all day?" Nate asked, and I leaned forward and smacked him on the side of the head.

"Hey. No violence. You just said you needed energy."

"I suddenly got the energy," I said deadpan and then ducked out of the way of Nate's fist as I made my way to the master bath.

Nate went to the guest room, and I figured he would at least shower and change into the clothes he'd brought.

I liked that our family was so close. We weren't spread across the US like so many others. It'd be nice if our parents lived closer, but our dad's job had transferred him, and now they were happy out there. I didn't get to see them enough, but at least I had my siblings.

I showered quickly, knowing if I didn't move my ass, I wouldn't be able to have a cup of coffee before I left for work. I didn't know why I was so nervous. It wasn't like I didn't see Paris often. Was she making me nervous? What were we going to say to each other when we saw each other next?

I was also worried because I had no idea what the fuck Benji was going to do.

He hadn't said a word about the attack. Unlike the others in the office. They'd been carefully quiet about it, only murmuring to each other. I didn't think anyone thought anyone in the office had done it, but it still felt as if we were all scared to mention it.

Could it happen to them? Or was someone out to get Paris?

Or maybe I was wrong, and they were all talking about it behind my back in louder tones. That could well be the case.

I would've thought they would talk to me to figure out what I knew. The others at the branch hadn't done that, but that meant I didn't know what they all likely thought. I was only a visitor in their world, after all. My time with the branch was short, and then I would move on back to my old office, most likely with a promotion if things worked out well with the project.

And I would no longer be working daily with Paris.

I didn't want to think about what that meant because once I wasn't working with her anymore, maybe we could start something.

"Fuck." I bashed my knee into the cabinet as I got out of the shower.

I did not need to think about that. I would not be dating Paris. No matter what. There were rules. We were friends. Nothing more.

Now that the idea was in my mind, I didn't know what to think.

Nate was gone by the time I came out of my room, ready for work. Nate only had to get dressed in his casual clothes since he wasn't working today, but I had to put on my tie and everything.

There was a note by the coffee maker, and my travel mug filled to the brim with steaming brew.

Say hi to Paris for me.

I grinned at his note, picked up my coffee, and made my way to my car.

I would act natural.

Act as if nothing had happened. Maybe that was wrong. And I had a feeling I wasn't going to be able to do that, but Paris would make it through this and come out the other side as strong as ever. She was going to be okay, and me focusing on it would make it difficult for both of us. So, I would follow her lead and bring it up only if she wanted to talk.

I hoped.

I pulled into the parking lot, my hands fisting on the steering wheel as I did.

Paris wasn't here yet, but I parked where I normally did, not sure if she would park close to her old spot where the attack had happened, or pick a new one. It didn't matter, though, because I would be walking her to her car.

So, apparently, I wasn't going to act as if nothing had happened.

Even though there were now cameras in the parking lot, the new technology wouldn't protect Paris if someone came at her again.

I was not going to react the same as I had before the attack. I was going to do my best to make sure she was safe.

And deal with her yelling and the other frustrating consequences.

I got to my office without seeing anybody, grateful because I wasn't in the mood to chat.

Anxiety and stress filled my gut, and I hated it.

I just needed to focus on work, and when the time came, see what Paris wanted to do. There wasn't much else I could do.

When everyone started showing up for work, the buzz in the office was different, and I knew they were all waiting for Paris to come in.

Hell, she was going to hate arriving to find this. She

would want to do her best to not be the center of attention, and it was going to be the exact opposite of that.

When people started talking a little louder, and I could tell they were in groups, I stood up from my desk and walked out to the hallway, doing my best to act nonchalant.

I was failing like everyone else.

The elevator dinged, and Paris walked onto the floor, her chin held high, and a scarf around her neck. I knew it was to cover the bruises. I had seen the red marks when I picked her up from the gravel, trying to see if she was awake and alive.

She didn't smile at anyone but gave them nods, and nobody came up to her, but they did look a little scared as if they didn't know what to do.

Well, they weren't alone in that.

Benji was nowhere to be seen, and I was grateful for that.

I leaned against my door, waiting for her to pass. When she did, she gave me a small smile and went straight to her office.

When she didn't close the door behind her, everybody was quiet, staring at me, and I shrugged, knowing I would have to be the one to break the ice.

Nobody knew what to do here, and by the looks on their faces, most of them wanted to say something to reassure her. Nobody seemed malicious or mean, at least.

I would do something. Because while nobody seemed mean, they also looked as if they wanted to help and had no idea how to do it.

Maybe for someone else, they'd have made coffee or gotten her breakfast or gone to hug her.

But this was Paris.

And she was a little prickly.

I was used to that.

So I pulled myself from my office and made the trek to hers.

I stood in the doorway, my hands in my pockets, and stared at her as she stood in front of her desk, her shoulders rising as she took deep breaths.

"Hey," I said.

She whirled around, her eyes wide, and dropped her briefcase.

"Fuck," I muttered under my breath, then took three steps towards her, my hands outstretched. I didn't touch her, and I was grateful I didn't because she flinched.

That reaction sent rage through me, and I wanted to hurt someone. I wanted to scream. I didn't. Thankfully, I knew that nobody was looking inside the room, because they wouldn't dare.

I also didn't close the door because I didn't want to

have any more attention focused on this than there already was. I was already fucking things up.

"Sorry. You startled me."

"I should've knocked instead of walking right in." I let out a breath.

"Hi."

"Hi."

We were both kneeling now, picking up the papers that had fallen out of her briefcase. I looked at her, at the dark circles under her eyes, even if they had been carefully covered with concealer. I wanted to punch someone.

"I'm glad you're back," I said, the only thing I could say just then.

Surprise covered her face for an instant, and then she smiled. That Paris smile that I loved. The one that wasn't the icy façade that she shrouded herself in to be strong.

No, it was the smile that she showed her friends when no one else was looking.

I wasn't sure I'd ever seen that expression directed at me before.

"I'm glad I'm back, too. I want normal. Although I don't know if it can be that way when it comes to this office."

"You have a bunch of socially inept people who don't know how to talk to one another, trying to figure out how to help you."

"I know. I just hate being the center of attention."

We both stood up, and I handed her the rest of her papers, careful not to touch her.

"You know if they knew what to do, you would have muffins or scones or coffee or something on your desk."

"They sent flowers and cards."

"I know," I said, putting my hands in my pockets again.

"The people here can be kind. At least, most of them."

"He's not here today," I said softly.

Her shoulders fell, but it was more like a balloon with air being released, more from tension than disappointment.

"That's good. I didn't want to deal with him."

"Me, either."

"And I can't believe I said that."

"You're allowed to say it. Anyway, you're the one who sets the tone so that you can act normal, and people will eventually act normal, as well. Or you can talk about it. It's up to you, but we're here, no matter what."

I didn't mean to become the spokesman for a company that I wasn't going to be with long, but here I was.

"Thanks, Prior." She let out a breath, and I steeled myself because I had no idea what she was going to say next. "Can we go out for a drink after this?" she asked.

"Well, more like coffee or something since I shouldn't be drinking alcohol."

"Are you okay?" I asked quickly, worry filling me.

"I'm fine. I'm just on concussion protocol, and I shouldn't add booze to my system. Even though I should be able to drink again soon."

"Oh, that's good," I said awkwardly.

"I could use a martini."

"A martini sounds great," I said, even though it was only eight in the morning.

She laughed then, and I laughed with her.

"Anyway, if you're too busy, or if you have a date with Allison or something, no worries. I just figured, well...anyway."

"Allison and I broke up," I said quickly, not sure why I'd brought it up.

Her eyes widened.

"Oh?" she asked, her throat working as she swallowed hard.

"It's over. I'll tell you what happened later. If you want." I let out a breath. "Anyway, it's not a big deal. We can get coffee or a smoothie or something after work."

"Or, I don't know, I want a place where I can say thank you without feeling awkward. And I think that, no matter what, it's going to be awkward."

I froze, not knowing what to say.

"Seriously. Thank you. I have no idea what would've happened if you hadn't been there. And I don't want to think about it. I don't want to talk about any of it ever again. However, I figured I at least owed you a drink."

"We can do that. And maybe another time if you're going to be too tired after today." I said that quickly and winced.

"You know, you're right," she said with a laugh, surprising me. "As soon as I said it, I was a little worried because I just want to go home and go to bed."

I shook my head. "Let's raincheck then."

I looked at her, wondering what the fuck I was doing. I had no idea what was going on in my brain, but what I did know was that whatever path my mind wanted to go down wasn't the right path for me. And it sure as fuck wasn't the right path for her.

"Raincheck it is. Thank you. Seriously. And one day, maybe I'll want to talk about it some more, but not right now. I want to go to work. I want to look at details, and I want to tell you that you're wrong a lot," she said with a laugh, and I snorted.

"Now that is the Paris we missed."

"Damn straight," she said, and then we were silent, looking at each other, the quiet filling the room. I swallowed hard before lifting my chin and walking out.

And I knew that no matter what happened next, we needed to be careful.

Because I could not fuck up my friendship with her, however tentative and weird it was.

She had been through enough, and I didn't want to hurt her any more than she already was.

As I made my way to my office, I knew that my mind wasn't going to let it rest.

The word *complicated* was only the beginning.

Chapter 10

Paris

I LICKED MY LIPS AND PROWLED ACROSS THE ROOM. Prior sat on the couch, his legs spread, his jeans unzipped. He rubbed himself over the cotton of his boxer briefs, staring at me, his mouth parted, his eyes dark.

All I wore were high heels that I didn't even remember buying, tiny lace panties that barely covered anything, and a smile.

Or perhaps it was a smirk.

My breasts swayed with each movement I made, my hips sashaying just as hard.

I kept moving, one step at a time.

And then I was on my knees in front of him, his hand

pulling at my hair as I gripped the base of him, his large cock too big for my hands, the tip of it grazing my lips.

"Suck it, Paris."

"Is that an order? I thought I was the one who told you what to do."

"Open."

I opened, and he slid his cock between my lips. I gasped, swallowing him whole as his dick touched the back of my throat. I nearly gagged but relaxed my muscles to take more of him in, and then he was pulling at my hair so hard that it almost hurt. Only I couldn't feel a thing.

Odd.

He fucked my mouth, lifting his hips off the couch as I dug my nails into his thighs and then removed one hand so I could grip his balls, playing with him, kneading him, trying to touch every bit of him.

And then I took a deep breath and was bent over the couch, his cock sliding in, hard and deep as he thrust into me, his dick warm and thick and stretching me. He had his hands in my hair, tugging again, and then they were on my hips, my breasts, pinching and plucking and sending me right over the edge.

And then I was on my back, the gravel digging into my skin, blood trickling from little cuts all over my body. Prior was above me, thrusting inside of me, and then he wasn't there. Instead, there was someone else, someone in the shadows, their hands around my throat. I woke up with a scream, wondering what the fuck had just happened.

My hands were between my legs, and I grimaced, pulling them away, noticing how wet I was.

Great, I had gotten myself off in my dreams, thinking about Prior of all people, and had somehow ended it all with a twist that I did not want to think about.

I wasn't afraid of Prior. Far from it. My brain wanted to mix things up to the point that I felt sick.

I still didn't know who had hurt me, and I didn't like that that was what I was thinking about right then.

It'd ruined a perfectly good sex dream.

A fantasy so real, my thighs ached from it.

I wanted to go back to it and remember what he'd felt like when he was inside of me.

Then I shook myself out of that thought and cursed.

"I do not want to fuck Prior Brady."

If I said those words enough, maybe I would get it through my skull that fucking Prior would be a bad thing.

I let out a breath and then rolled out of bed, tugging my sheets off the mattress. I would wash them and get the smell of sex out of my room since I could practically taste Prior on my lips.

No, that would not be happening.

Just because I had a slight attraction to the man, didn't mean I needed to fuck him. It would be too complicated.

I was going to find another date so I could get over him, even though I had told myself I wouldn't go on another date.

Well, that was clearly going to be thrown out the window. The girls would have to find me someone. Someone who wasn't Prior.

Because we worked together.

At least, for the time being. Though his time with my branch of the company was coming to an end. Soon, he would leave, and that obstacle would no longer be in the way.

There would be plenty of other obstacles, though.

Namely the fact that we didn't always like each other. And even though he didn't have a girlfriend now, he had only recently gotten out of a semi-serious relationship.

Not that he seemed too broken up about it.

It wasn't my place to judge. I didn't have a right to do that. For all I knew, he was breaking inside and simply putting on a brave face because he worried that I would feel bad or something.

After all, he kept watching me as if I would shatter at any minute.

I didn't blame him. He'd seen me bleeding. Had saved my life.

I never wanted to be indebted to anyone, let alone the man I had sex dreams about.

No, I could not have another fantasy about him. I could not think about him in that way.

He was part of our core group, the new one that we'd somehow formed when Cross and Hazel got together.

I couldn't break those connections and make things awkward by wanting to fuck him.

Or wanting to hold him.

Wanting to get to know him.

No, none of that. Ever.

I was not going to think about Prior.

My phone buzzed as I stuffed my pajamas and sheets into the washer, not caring if I had to mix them. I looked down at it, standing naked in my laundry room, and cursed.

Great, of course.

Prior: *Hey, just seeing how you're doing. You didn't talk to me much this week, and I wanted to make sure you were feeling okay.*

"I didn't talk to you because I'm avoiding you. I'm not going to use the word avoiding because that would make you matter."

And now I was standing naked in my laundry room and talking to myself while looking at a text from a man I'd just had a weird sex dream about.

I had reached a new level of insanity, and I wasn't

quite sure what to do now that I was in this new circle of hell.

I let out a breath and answered him.

Me: *I'm fine. Just doing some laundry.*

That wasn't a lie. I wouldn't tell him that I was doing laundry because every time I looked at my sheets, I thought about wrapping my lips around his cock. But then again, we hadn't been in my bedroom, we had been on my couch.

Could I wash my couch? Or maybe burn it?

I would have to get a whole new couch, but that was fine. Maybe then I wouldn't have sex dreams about Prior on that one.

Images of a sofa I had never seen before filled my mind with me bent over the back of it as Prior slammed into me.

Great, great, great.

Now I was having daydreams about fucking Prior.

I needed to get that out of my mind. Maybe rub one out to Channing Tatum or someone.

Was Channing Tatum the current hot guy?

No, Oscar Isaac. Oscar Isaac would be the one I would have daydreams about.

And his hair sort of looked like Prior's with the way it curled right at his neck and temples.

What the hell, Paris?

I growled and looked at my phone as it pinged again.

Prior: *If you say so. Well, I'm around this weekend if you need anything.*

"Why would I need anything? Why is he being so nice?"

I needed to stop talking to myself.

Me: *Thanks. Just doing housework. See you on Monday.*

Prior: *Good deal.*

He didn't say anything more, and I was grateful. After all, I was losing my mind, and I had no idea what I was supposed to do.

I did my best to push thoughts of Prior from my mind and made my way to my bathroom, ignoring my reflection in the mirror. I didn't like to look at the bruises still healing on my skin.

I had always bruised easily, and the attack had just made that even more evident. I was healing, but my skin was taking its sweet time.

It didn't help that every time that I dreamed about falling, I always remembered the exact feel of the gravel against my flesh. That wasn't something I ever wanted to feel again, but my dreams weren't letting me forget it.

I quickly showered and then went about my business, putting on creams and doing my hair. I wanted to feel pretty, or at least normal. I had nowhere to go today, but having my hair done so I wouldn't have to wash it the next day was pretty much the main reason for doing that and taking the time.

I had been truthful when I'd told Prior I didn't have anything to do today, so I pulled out my tablet and looked through my house to-do list. I went through what I needed to clean and deep clean and figured I could do that for the day, and then winced when I looked at what was overdue.

"Fuck."

I needed to replace the filter in my A/C unit. The only problem? It was in the attic. Why they had put it in the attic at a hard angle was beyond me. In fact, it was one of those tiny ones that was one foot by one foot and barely did anything.

I hated it, but it'd come with the house. And with my current rib situation, and the pain I was already in from healing, I knew I wouldn't be able to do it. Not that I'd ever done it on my own before, but that was a whole other matter.

"Fuck," I mumbled again.

And while I could maybe use my little, rickety ladder to get up into the attic, if I got hurt again—and I probably would since the last time I had tripped over the bottom step, I had fallen and bruised my elbow—my friends would hurt me more.

And while I wanted to do everything on my own most of the time, I was trying to lean on others more.

Because my ribs already hurt, I pulled out my phone and dialed.

"Hey there," Hazel said.

"Hey," I said. "I need some help."

"You're asking for help? Are you okay?" Hazel asked, and I could tell that she had just stood up as if she were ready to grab her keys and head to me.

"I'm fine. I'm not hurt. However, I do need some help changing the air filter in my attic. I have a spare one. I have two actually, but I can't physically do it right now. And as much as I loathe saying it, I could use either your or Cross's help."

"I can do that for sure. I'm actually with Cross's family's family at the moment, but we can make this work."

"His family's family?" I asked, somewhat confused. Then again, I did get confused with the number of people Cross knew.

"Cross's sister's family. A few of us are hanging out, but I can head over. Or I can send Cross or someone. One of the Montgomerys."

I had heard of the Montgomerys, and had even almost gone on a blind date with the last single one, but that hadn't happened. I was grateful because one didn't date within one's circle, even if that circle was sort of somewhat adjacent to ours.

"Take your time. Or do it this weekend. Or next weekend. I don't know, I'll think of something."

"No, I'm sending someone right now. Do not get up on that ladder. If you do, I will know, and if you get hurt, it will not be me who hurts you more. Or even Myra. No, I'll send the mother. Dakota will strip your hide. She's a mom. She knows how to give you that *I'm disappointed in you* look that makes you feel even worse than if she'd actually yelled at you."

That made me smile and wince at nearly the same time. "You're right. She does do that whole *I'm disappointed* look, doesn't she?"

"I hear you learn it during the birthing process, or at least during the first few months."

"When you and Cross have a baby, you can tell me all about it."

"Okay, slow your roll. We are not having kids anytime soon."

"So you say. You're the one who told me you try to jump his bones as much as you can."

"And there are such things as condoms."

"Condoms break. Babies are born. And I want to be an auntie again. So get on that." I paused, grinned. "Or get on *him*, I should say."

"You know I'm trying to do you a favor, and now you're making me picture having sex with my man." She paused. "Well, I'm going to hate you for that only because I'm surrounded by other people, but I'm going to thank you for it later."

"Great, now *I'm* picturing it," I lied.

"Stop picturing Cross naked."

Sadly, it wasn't Cross who came to mind all naked and hard and wanting.

No, it was his brother.

Fuck. I was so screwed.

Or rather, *not* screwed.

"Thank you for sending someone. And jump his bones later. Only not in public. I don't want to have to bail you out of jail."

"You're so sweet. Love you."

"Love you, too."

I ended the call, and then let out a breath, doing my best to slow my racing heart because I kept thinking about Prior in ways I shouldn't.

I was losing my mind, and I didn't know what to do about it.

I knew I could count on Hazel, so I went back to my to-do list and got started on a few other things I could do around the house while waiting to see who she sent me.

I was out on the back porch, sweeping off the old

leaves and dirt that had gotten there thanks to the wind, and froze, looking over my shoulder.

Why did it feel like someone was watching me? There were trees behind my house and a large fence that nobody could see through since it was made of metal and adobe. I was grateful for where my house was located in the subdivision because I was on the end, and it was hard for anybody to see through my windows or anything like that. It was one of the main reasons for my purchase.

But it felt like somebody was watching me.

Dread rolled in my belly, and the hair on my neck stood on end, so I quickly swept the rest of the porch, trying not to let my paranoia ruin my day. Then I went back into my house, locking all the doors.

I went as far as closing the blinds on that side of the house. I let out a deep breath, telling myself that I was just overreacting.

Nobody was watching me.

It wasn't as if anyone could be.

Then I remembered the attack, and the fact that my dad was out, and my mom.

Maybe somebody was watching.

I almost called my detective, but I didn't want to bother him.

Before I could wrestle with that decision, someone

knocked on the door, and I froze before shaking myself out of my reverie and walking towards the front of the house.

I looked through the peephole and could have cursed.

Of course.

Of course.

I unlocked the deadbolt and the other two locks before opening the door to Prior.

He stood there, his hands in his pockets, his hair looking a little windblown, and the stubble on his face looking way too sexy.

I wanted to reach out and touch that chest of his, to see if it was as hard as it looked. I wanted to go up on my tiptoes and bite at his chin, just nibble and taste and lick.

I was losing my mind.

And I needed to stop doing that.

"Hey. Hazel said you needed help?"

"Yes, I do."

I wasn't going to sound awkward at all, was I?

"I asked if you needed help earlier. You could have texted me."

I narrowed my eyes and then folded my arms over my chest. I didn't realize that I had just made my breasts look larger and more pressed together until I saw his gaze drop and then quickly move back up to my eyes.

Or maybe I imagined it.

"I didn't know I needed help when you asked, and

then I reached out to Hazel because she usually knows who to contact. Or Myra or Dakota. I'm used to talking to them."

I shook my head and then took a step back, lowering my arms to gesture for him to come inside.

"Anyway, though, thank you. My unit is in the attic, and I can't get to it."

"Why do they put them in the attic?" he asked, shaking his head.

He smelled like cedar and male.

Dear God, I had it bad.

"I don't know, but it's very annoying. I pulled out my car earlier since the access is in the garage, so let me open the garage door and show you how to get up there."

"No problem," Prior said, looking around my house.

I followed his gaze. "It's not much, and I'm still figuring out how I want to decorate, but I like it."

"It looks great," Prior said. "I'm not good at decorating, so I pretty much have random things that I've seen and liked over the years, and it's sort of made this whole metal and wood thing."

"My house is white and gray with splashes of wine because I like wine, and that's the color that Myra gave me, and I went with it."

Prior laughed. "Maybe I need to get Myra to decorate part of my house."

I didn't want to think of Myra and Prior together, and I didn't know why I was so jealous right then. What was wrong with me?

We went out to the garage, and I opened the big door, and he stood under the hatch to the attic and looked up.

"How the hell do you reach this?"

"A ladder and a prayer?" I asked.

"Are you asking me or telling me?"

"I don't know. I usually just jump like a duck or something."

"Now I'm imagining it, with your limbs all flailing about."

"Stop it," I said with a laugh.

He reached out, hopped a little bit, his toes barely lifting off the floor, and grabbed the cord.

"Showoff," I said.

"Yes, it's the height. I work hard at it. You got that filter?" he asked.

"Yes, let me get it," I said, going to the shelving unit where it was stored in a large black bag so it wouldn't get wet.

I handed it over to him, and he crawled up the ladder. I winced at how flimsy it was.

"You need better brackets on this."

"It came with the house, and I've never been up there

other than the first time during the inspection. I never want to do it again."

"How have you changed your filter before?"

"I sort of just ask friends to help. Or my neighbor. Or a handyman once, but that cost me an arm and a leg."

I did my best to keep my eyes off Prior's very nice ass as he ascended the ladder, but I failed.

I couldn't help it. He filled out his jeans so perfectly.

I clearly needed to go on another date, but not with him. This was going too far.

"Almost done," he called out, and I looked up at the hole in the ceiling and hoped he would get down soon and then leave so I wouldn't have to look at him anymore. Or think about him the way I kept doing.

Not that I needed him to be here for me to think about him like that.

He made his way down the ladder, and I winced when it started to squeak.

"Get off that, I don't want you to fall."

I must have startled him, and his forearms bulged as he held himself tight to the ladder, having missed three rungs above the bottom.

My pulse raced, and I reached forward, holding out my hands to stop him from falling.

Only my hands were on his ass and not on the rest of him. My face burned.

Prior looked over his shoulder, his brows raised. I quickly lowered my hands, my heart beating so quickly that I could actually hear it pulsing in my ears. And then he was off the ladder, standing in front of me, his chest heaving.

"Sorry for touching you. For your butt. Well, not sorry for your butt. Because you have a great butt. I just wanted to let you know that I'm sorry for touching that part of you, but...thank you. Because I couldn't have done that on my own."

"Are you done?" he asked, and my brows rose.

"No need to be rude. I said I was sorry."

"You don't need to be sorry." He let out a breath. "I only wanted to make sure you were done talking."

"What do you mean?"

"This is what I mean."

And then I thought I was dreaming again. Prior's hand was in my hair, and his mouth was on mine. I couldn't breathe.

Though I didn't think I needed air again if I had this.

Chapter 11

Prior

I SHOULD NOT BE DOING THIS.

I was doing it anyway.

I angled her head and kissed her deeper, her taste a sin on my tongue as if it were everything I had been missing.

Dear God. I needed to stop. We needed to talk about this.

Talk? Who the fuck was I?

She slid her tongue against mine, and I groaned, needing more.

Her hands were on my chest, her nails digging in. Not pulling me closer, but not pushing me away.

I didn't know what to do. I knew what I needed to do,

what would be smart for both of us. We needed to stop this, walk away, and pretend it never happened.

I knew that wouldn't be what I did.

Because, apparently, I was good at making mistakes, and this was a whopper.

I pulled away, gasping for breath as she did the same, then I rested my forehead against hers. Her fingernails still dug into my skin through my shirt, her hands clasping once, twice, before she relaxed a bit, nearly letting go. She didn't push me away, though.

Instead, I was the one who moved away, taking a step back, lowering my hands so I could see her.

"Well," I said, knowing I should probably have said something better than that. What was there to say?

"*Well.* That's a good word for it. The other words would likely be a little more profane, so, *well* works."

I smiled that that, not able to help myself.

"It's pretty much what I was thinking."

"I didn't ask you over for that." She frowned. "I didn't ask you over at all, actually."

"I know. I didn't come here thinking this would happen." I paused, kind of frowning. "I'm not going to lie and say I haven't thought about it, though."

Her eyes widened, and I wanted to take my foot out of my mouth and apologize.

"You've thought about this?" she asked.

"All the fucking time, Paris. And we both know it would be a mistake to take it further. *This* is probably a mistake."

It didn't take a genius to see the hurt cross her face. I wanted to kick myself.

"Not that I think the kiss was a mistake. I meant how it *could* be."

"Your semantics don't make sense," she bit out through gritted teeth.

"You're right. They don't. Because I've been doing my best *not* to think about you."

"Right back at you. You shouldn't be here. You shouldn't have come at all. You shouldn't have kissed me. Or I shouldn't have let you kiss me. Whatever."

"Why?" I asked.

"You're the one who called it a mistake. You tell *me* why."

"I wanted to make sure we were on the same page for why this is wrong."

"Wrong. Mistake. Seems you're good at using the words that push me away. You won. Now, go."

"We need to talk about this, Paris."

"No, we don't. You've talked enough for both of us."

"I'm not saying the right things, and I'm sorry. How could I tell you that I've been thinking about this a lot?

We fucking work together. So as long as I'm there, I shouldn't be doing this."

"There's nothing in our bylaws that says it's against the rules."

She said the words so low that I almost missed them.

"You looked that up?"

"Of course, I did," she bit out and then turned away, beginning to pace before she spoke again.

"I'm an idiot. You're right. This is a mistake."

"It's not against the rules?"

"No, it's not. I already have to deal with Benji and his ilk. This isn't smart."

"I never said I was smart."

"So you're calling me stupid right along with you?" she asked.

"Paris."

She rolled on me, her eyes dark as she narrowed her gaze at me. "You kissed me. You got it out of your system. We shouldn't do it again."

"That doesn't mean we can't," I said slowly.

"Wouldn't, shouldn't, couldn't, can't, all the words we can mix together. They're still not going to make any sense."

"Paris. The main reason for us not to is our friends."

"I know that. It's why you should leave. We should just forget that this ever happened."

Dread filled my belly, but I nodded.

"I don't want to go."

"Why? Do you want to hurt them?"

"No, I don't. But it's so confusing."

"You just got out of a relationship, too. A pretty serious one."

"She was fucking her ex in *my* bed. I'm pretty sure it wasn't that serious."

Her eyes widened, and she took a step forward.

"Prior."

"No, I don't need any sympathy. Only wanted to let you know exactly what happened. There's no going back. And honestly, right now, she's not a part of this."

"Maybe she should be."

"No, she shouldn't. She can do whatever she wants, and so can we."

"Prior," she said again.

"We're going to talk about this. We're going to figure this out. Because that kiss? You know we can't ignore it."

"Maybe it'd be smarter if we did."

"Are you going to tell the girls?"

"We try not to keep secrets from each other. However, if this is just a one-time thing, maybe I shouldn't tell them at all. That way, it's not a big deal."

I moved forward and traced her jaw with my finger.

She didn't move away. I moved my hand so I could cover her cheek.

"What if it's not a one-time thing, Paris?" I asked, the tension between us palpable. I still had her taste on my lips, and I wanted to kiss her again. Needed to touch her, to know what she felt like.

I wanted so much, yet I knew I was being a selfish dick. I didn't care.

Or maybe, I cared too much. Perhaps that was the problem.

"I don't know, give me time." She paused. "Are you going to tell your brothers?"

"I might. I talk to them when I get frustrated and I can't think through things."

"Oh, if you do, then I guess it's going to be a thing in our group regardless."

"Well, if you talk to the girls, and it becomes a thing, maybe we should see what happens."

"I need time to think, Prior. Can you give me that?"

I nodded, lowering my hand. "Of course. Anything you need, Paris."

"And that's the problem," she said softly. "I think you know exactly what I need."

And on that note, I wasn't sure what else there was to say, so I turned on my heel and left the house. I heard the lock snick behind me, all three of them, and I was glad that she was making herself safe.

Because even with all the heat between us, the tension that rolled through my belly and slid up my spine, there was still the fact that someone had hurt her. And we didn't know who it was.

That hadn't left my mind the entire time I was with her, and the idea of Paris getting hurt again made me want to go down to knees and pray.

As I started my car and pulled away, I knew where I needed to go.

My brothers could help me.

Even if I didn't know what to say to them.

Since I knew that Cross and Hazel were still at Arden's, I went to the next closest house, Macon's. If he wasn't there, I'd try Nate. I could text them or call and tell them I was coming, but I needed to get my thoughts in order first.

Thankfully, Macon's truck was out front when I pulled in. It looked like it had recently been washed.

I pulled in next to his vehicle, got out of the car, and headed towards the open garage where my brother was standing, looking over his workbench and frowning.

"Hey," I said softly, trying not to startle him. Apparently, not well enough. Macon twisted on his feet, fists ready, and punched out. I ducked in time not to get hit in the nose, but he got me in the shoulder. I bent over, cursing.

"Fuck," I cried out.

"Shit. Sorry, man. Don't scare me like that. Hell. I'm sorry. You okay?" Macon started rambling and stuffed his hands into his jeans' pockets, rocking back on his heels.

I nodded, rubbed my shoulder, and looked at my sibling.

He was pale, his face sweat-slick, and I had a feeling that had just happened in the two seconds since I came up and scared him.

"I'm fine," I said. But I knew my brother *wasn't* okay.

And I had no idea what to do about it.

I'd almost lost both of my brothers that day when they got shot, and while Cross had Hazel to lean on and seemed to act like nothing had happened, Macon was doing his best to pretend like everything was okay, to the point that it was all a lie.

I didn't know what to do to protect my brother.

"I need to get better at ducking," I said, trying to laugh it off. I didn't know what else to do or say. Macon studied my face for a long moment before giving me a tight nod.

"Sorry. You just startled me. You want a beer?" he asked, and I looked down at my watch, noting that it was after two. I nodded.

"A beer sounds delicious."

I followed Macon into the house, stepping out of the way so he could close the garage door behind us.

"Did I interrupt something?" I asked.

"No, just reorganizing the garage."

Considering that Macon had bowed out of going with Arden, I had hoped it had been for a good reason, but I guess not wanting to be around crowds made sense. I knew that Nate had been working this morning and hadn't been able to make it, but Macon hadn't come up with an excuse. I wanted to know what the hell was wrong with my baby brother.

I just didn't think this was the right time to ask. He would come to us if he needed us.

I only hoped it wouldn't be too late.

"So, what can I help you with?" Macon asked. I kind of wished I hadn't come. Because I didn't want to bother Macon with my petty problems, not when I knew that he had his own healing to do. Maybe him worrying about my issues would help him get over what the fuck was going on in his own mind.

Or maybe I just needed to talk with someone.

"I kissed Paris," I blurted.

Macon choked on his beer, spewing liquid every-where, and I wiped my face and took a step back.

"Thanks for that."

"Fuck. Warn me next time."

I set down my beer, laughing as I shook my head. I stripped off my shirt, wiped my face, and threw the bundled material at him.

"Asshole," I said with a laugh.

"I don't know, I've never actually done a spit take like that before."

I met Macon's gaze, and we both burst out laughing. I followed him back to the guest room where I kept a few shirts and odds and ends.

"I think I have an old AC/DC shirt of yours."

"Wouldn't that be Cross's?"

"Maybe. I don't know. We're all about the same size. Hopefully, it still fits."

He searched through his drawers and handed over the black T-shirt with the familiar logo. I went to wash my face before I slid the tee over my head, still feeling like I smelled like beer.

"So. You and Paris?" Macon asked from the doorway, folding his arms over his chest.

"I think so."

"What's there to think about? She's hot, and you're okay."

"Thanks. I truly appreciate it."

"No problem. Seriously, what's there to think about?"

"How about the fact that she's friends with Hazel, and now part of our new group."

"And we can't date within the group?" he asked, his voice a little too casual. I wasn't going to touch on that, because frankly, I had my own shit to worry about.

"Well, we shouldn't. Right?"

"I don't know. You guys are always shooting daggers at each other, isn't that chemistry supposed to be hot or something?"

"That's where you're going with this?"

He threw his hands up in disgust and walked away from me as I followed him back into the kitchen. He got himself another beer since the first one was now too flat since he'd shaken it.

"You know what? I don't know. You guys have chemistry, or whatever the hell you two have. If you're worried about hurting her? Then don't date her. You don't want to have to deal with Dakota and the bunch if you fuck her over."

I didn't fail to notice the fact that he had said Dakota rather than Hazel, but I wasn't going to mention it.

If I had sparks or angry chemistry with Paris, his with Dakota was tenfold. I didn't think any of us dared to comment on it. At least, not yet.

"I don't want to screw things up, mess them up, or ruin anything."

"Those all mean the same thing," Macon said.

"See? I'm so flustered, I don't know how to speak."

"Okay, what's making you not want to do this?"

"I don't want to hurt her."

"Not a good enough reason. You don't want to hurt anyone you're in a relationship with, even Allison. Even though she cheated on you."

"Fine," I said, sighing.

"If things get weird between Paris and me, I don't want them to be weird in the group."

"The girls don't hang out with us all the time, and it's not like she used to date one of us or anything. We have other friends. We can make this work. And as long as you don't screw her over or hurt her too badly, it won't be a problem. And you wouldn't do that. You're a good guy."

That warmed me, and I grinned. "Thanks."

"You're welcome. Now I'm going to flip you off so we stop being all warm and brotherly." He flipped me off, and I grinned, liking that he was a bit back to his old self, even though I knew the tension running just under the surface was about ready to explode at any minute.

I only hoped to hell that one of us was there when it happened.

I didn't want him to be alone.

"What else?" Macon asked, pulling me out of my thoughts.

"We work together."

"That could be an issue."

"However, she said that she looked it up and it's not against the rules. Plus, I won't be there for much longer."

Macon grinned, his eyes bright. "She looked it up?"

"Yes," I said, grinning right back.

"Well. It's not like you guys are going to flaunt it at work anyway. So, I don't think that's going to be a big deal. Just don't fuck her on your desk at work and you'll be fine."

Now, images of that filled my mind, and I let out an oof as Macon punched me in my other shoulder.

"Stop thinking about it. Because then that image is going to get inside my mind, and I don't have any bleach right now to take care of it."

"Hey, you're the one who said it."

"And I regret it already."

"Anyway, I don't know."

"You're never going to know if you keep pussyfooting around it."

"You're so good with the words, so wise and sage."

"You came to me, not Cross or even Hazel."

"Make that Arden."

"I noticed you didn't mention Nate."

"Why would I mention him?" Macon asked, and I laughed.

"He's not here to defend himself. Don't be mean." I sighed.

"I don't know what to do," I whispered.

"Yes, you do. Take a chance. You never know when you're going to get another."

I frowned, looking at Macon, wondering what to say. "Are you okay?" I asked, the words leaving my mouth before I'd even fully thought them.

Macon froze for a bare instant, but I saw it. The fear, the stress, the worry.

And I didn't know how to help.

"Everything's fine. Just waiting to see what happens between you and Paris. Y'all are starting to get paired off. Eventually, Nate will find someone, and then hell will freeze over."

I wanted to say: *What about you?*

I didn't ask though, because he had purposely not mentioned himself, and I wasn't going to push. Not now.

"So, can I have another beer?" I asked, and Macon's shoulders lowered a bit, relief covering him.

I wasn't going to broach the subject, not again, at least not for now.

I had my second beer, as well as a glass of water and dinner before I headed back home, feeling lighter, if a bit more worried about my brother. I was going to keep an eye on him, just like I knew the rest of my siblings would. And we'd be there when he needed us.

I only hoped to hell he reached out.

I pulled into my garage and got out of the car, rolling back my shoulders, knowing that I needed a little bit of courage to do what I was about to do next.

I let out a breath, got to my living room, and sat down on the couch, pulling out my phone.

Me: *I know we need to talk. How about we do that over dinner?*

I had been thinking about what I needed to say to her, and when I would reach out, and yet I wasn't very good at this.

The little bubble telling me she was messaging me back appeared almost immediately, and I didn't know whether to be relieved that she had seen the text, or worried that she was going to say no very quickly.

Paris: *Is that your weird way of asking me out?*

Me: *What's so weird about it?*

I hadn't been this nervous to ask someone out since I was a teenager, and even then, I'd had so many hormones and inexperience flooding through me that I had jumped headfirst into most things.

Paris: *You should probably work on your moves.*

Me: *Well, I could either ask you to teach me, or I could show you what my moves are in person.*

Paris: *That's a little smoother.*

Me: *So what do you say? Let me take you out.*

Paris: *And what if this is a mistake?*

I let out a breath, knowing that she was right.

Me: *Then we'll figure it out together.*

She was silent for so long, I was afraid she was going to say no or find a nice way to let me down easy.

I didn't want nice. I wanted Paris.

I laughed at that and hoped to hell I never said it aloud to her face. Because that had not come out right in my head.

Paris: *We'd better.*

Paris: *I expect romance, I'm just saying.*

Relief flooded through me, and my cock twitched at the thought of our date.

"Down boy," I muttered.

Me: *I can do that. I promise.*

Paris: *And a Brady always keeps his promises?*

Me: *Always.*

I set my phone down, waiting for her to respond back. We'd plan our date.

I only hoped to hell this wasn't another mistake.

Chapter 12

Prior

I WAS NERVOUS.

Why was I so nervous?

Could it be the fact that I was going on a date with a woman that I worked with, a woman who I thought I knew but still wanted to know better? Someone I couldn't stop thinking about?

Probably.

I needed to stop thinking so hard about this and let it flow. That's how we had gotten where we were today, by living in the moment, and simply being. If I kept overthinking things, I would only make everything worse.

I needed to be the old Prior, the one who dove headfirst into stuff and did what I needed to do.

Not this current version of myself, who got overly emotional and worried about everything.

I pulled into Paris's driveway and turned off the car before getting out. I let out a breath, wiping my hands down my pants since I was sweating, and rolled my shoulders back as if preparing to go to war.

I liked battling with Paris, but this wasn't going to be one, was it?

Or maybe it could be. That would be fun. We had chemistry, after all, and getting into a skirmish could be part of the game.

Not that I wanted to play a game with Paris.

I truly needed to stop thinking in circles.

I made my way to her front door and rang the doorbell, rocking back on my heels as I waited.

She opened the door, and I swallowed hard, unable to think clearly.

She had on a green dress, one not made of silk or cotton, but a blend of something that looked soft to the touch.

It had a low neckline, so low that I got a peek of her breasts. I did my best not to stare.

I wasn't a dick.

Even though my dick was the one thinking right now.

The dress was sleeveless and tied up at her shoulders,

then dipped into her waist before flaring out over her knees.

It looked amazing on her, the green the perfect complement to her eyes and the dark chestnut of her hair.

Her skin was pale in the moonlight, her lips a pinkish color, and her eyes were done up in a smoky way that I'd never seen on her before.

I had seen her in jeans, in work clothes, and in sundresses and leggings and the like when she was hanging out with the girls and us.

I had never seen Paris like this.

Oh, I had seen her on dates, two of them, actually, and she had looked fucking sexy then, but this? *This* was something different.

Maybe because I knew it was for me.

Or maybe I was self-centered, and this was all for her.

I would be the one sitting across from her, though.

I swallowed hard again and tried to speak. Only nothing came out.

"Are you just going to stand there?" Paris asked, and I looked up at her grin.

"Hey."

Smooth.

"Hey there, Brady. You like what you see?"

"You know I do." I cleared my throat. "So much in

fact that we should go before I take you back inside and see *exactly* what you're wearing under that dress."

"You sure feel high of yourself, don't you?" she asked.

"I would make a joke about feeling you instead, but how about I take you to dinner?"

She threw back her head and laughed, exactly what I was going for.

"So, these are your moves?" she asked as we got into my car.

"You like them?"

"They're okay."

"I guess I'll have to do better from here on out."

"I suppose you will," she said, and we went on to talk about work of all things, our conversation progressing easily as if we had done it a hundred times before.

We'd always been slightly caustic to one another, maybe just our large personalities clashing, but now it felt as if we knew each other a bit better.

I didn't know everything. I knew there were secrets, dark ones from the glimpses I had gotten, but it wasn't my right to know those. At least not yet.

I wanted to know. I wanted to know everything.

And that should have scared me far more than it did.

We made our way to the restaurant, a little chop-house that I liked to go to, one that Paris had mentioned before in passing. I knew she had been here, and it wasn't a place I had taken Allison. Not that I hadn't wanted to take her here, but it had never come up. I wanted my first date with Paris to be somewhere different than where I had taken Allison, and not the two places where I had caught Paris on really shitty blind dates.

"I love this place," Paris said as we took our seats and leaned back as the hostess handed us our menus.

"Your waiter will be right with you."

"Thank you," I said, and then the young woman winked at Paris, gave her a once-over, and I grinned.

"Stop it," Paris said, blushing all the way to her ears and down her chest.

It seemed she might just blush all over. That was interesting—something I would have to discover more of.

Down, boy.

"Well," I said, grinning.

"Shut up."

"I'm just saying. She's hot."

"Yes, and she's probably a good ten years too young for me."

"Maybe five, but not ten."

"I don't know if you're calling her older or me older."

"Neither. And, anyway, it's kind of nice to watch you blush like that. You've never gotten embarrassed in front of me before."

"I'm on a date with you. Nobody else is allowed to check me out."

"True, but you do look fucking hot in that dress."

She blushed again, and I smiled.

"Thanks, now I feel like I need to cover up."

"Don't. You look great." Besides, my dick would regret it.

"I had it in the back of my closet, and I figured I'd try it out. Only now, I feel exposed."

"You're covered. Don't worry about it. Seriously."

"Maybe. I don't usually dress like this. My typical attire is what you see me in at work."

"Same here, although mine's a little easier, I just added a jacket. I don't usually wear them every day at work."

"True, and you do clean up quite nicely."

"Thanks, I'll take the compliment."

"You know you're hot. I wouldn't be here if you weren't."

She said that so deadpan that I snorted before I laughed right as the waiter came to our table.

"Hello, welcome to Oscar's," the waiter began, and we listened to the specials, my stomach growling. I was starving, and thankfully this place, even if it was a little fancy, had decent-sized portions.

"That all sounds so good," Paris said as she looked

down at her menu after the waiter had left with our drink orders.

"I know. I love this place. And their portions are small enough that I could probably eat everything, yet big enough to be full."

"Oh, right, I forgot. I've been to a couple of places around here where they try to make it so fancy that you're pretty much just eating off a big tablespoon. And sometimes, the spoon isn't even that big."

"Oh, that place Fontanos or something? I went there with Allison." I cringed. "Sorry."

"Don't be sorry. You witnessed me on two of my horrible dates. You're welcome to mention the fact that you recently dated another woman. It'd be awkward if we purposely didn't mention her name."

"Well, I don't need to bring her up."

"Are you sure?"

"I'm sure."

"Okay...this is going to be very awkward then." She grinned over my shoulder, and I froze, wondering where in my past life I had gone wrong.

I turned to see Allison strolling towards us in a red dress cut out in strategic places. I hated to admit it, but she looked amazing.

Her ex, who was probably no longer her ex, was on her arm. They sauntered over.

"I see you finally took the plunge," Allison said, glaring daggers at us.

"Allison." I paused. "I didn't actually catch your name before," I said, apparently a little angrier than I thought I was.

"It's Tony."

"You don't need to talk to them. Seems they found exactly what they were looking for. Good luck to the two of you." Allison turned to Paris. "You're going to need it."

And then she turned away, dragging Tony with her. I turned to Paris, wincing.

"Sorry about that."

Paris pressed her lips together before bursting out laughing, her shoulders shaking. Others had already been staring at us, and now they were giving us weird looks before pointedly turning away.

"What is so funny?"

"Oh, just the fact that you witnessed me on two very horrible dates that were quite embarrassing, and now I got to be part of yours."

"I'm not dating Allison. I'm on a date with you. And in a new version of hell where my ex shows up randomly."

"Welcome to my horror of dating. I mean, it wouldn't be me on a date if things didn't go horribly wrong."

I reached across the table and gripped her hand.

"Nothing's gone wrong yet. Don't discount me right out of the gate."

She didn't move her hand back. Instead, she rubbed her thumb down my forefinger, frowning.

"I told you, I'm not good at this."

"The others didn't set you up with me. We set each other up."

"I guess this doesn't count as the pact then."

"We can make it count if that will appease your pact gods. And, frankly, I don't want to think about you going on another date while you're on a date with me. Call me a caveman."

"I wouldn't do that," she said with a laugh.

"Plus, the girls already know we're on a date, so there's no going back now."

"Macon knows, too. And if the girls know, so does Cross. And I'm sure Nate found out from one of the brothers or Arden."

"Maybe. It does sound like a very complicated web."

"Or perhaps it's because we have some great friends and family who care about us, who happen to know we're out together. And now we don't have to talk about them. We can order a very nice steak, and maybe a lobster, and split it to make our version of surf and turf, and then enjoy our date."

"I'm sold. But if you order your steak well-done, it's over."

"How dare you desecrate a cow like that?"

She laughed again, and when the waiter came back, we placed our order, and I leaned forward, looking at her.

She was beautiful, and I loved that she never toned it down, never hid her beauty. Only she didn't always vamp it up, at least at work.

I understood why she didn't, considering that Benji and the rest were jerks about it.

I liked that she had gone all out for our date, with the smoky eye and all the other stuff that women did.

When the meals came, we split them up, and I groaned at the first bite.

"You're pretty much going to have to roll me out of here."

"Can we roll each other? Is that possible? Oh my God, I forgot about the warmed butter. I forgot what spice they add to it. It's perfect."

"Then the other butter that they have too for the steak? I think my arteries are clogging just talking about it, but I don't care. Is it okay if we don't talk much while we eat?"

"It's fine. We already talked enough. Dig in."

We laughed, and still talked, but about nothing too important.

We didn't need to talk about our pasts, though I didn't have one worth noting. I was an open book, but I knew Paris had a past. I wasn't going to pry. At least, not yet. That's not what first dates were for.

By the time we finished dessert because, of course, we had to share some tiramisu, I was so full I wasn't sure I could fit into my car.

"That was so amazing," Paris said, rubbing her belly over her dress.

"Hell yeah, it was. I'm about to have to undo the top button of my pants, though."

I laughed when she blushed again and stopped rubbing her stomach.

"I guess the whole acting sexy or whatever thing on a date probably doesn't include eating your weight in lobster and steak."

"It could. I mean, we already know each other, at least well enough. We're past some of the weird and awkward firsts. At least the ones that you had on your blind dates."

"Nothing can be worse than those blind dates," Paris said.

"That is true. I mean, although the waitress did check you out, I wasn't going to invite her along for a threesome."

"Good, because then I'd have to hurt you, and that's a whole thing I wasn't in the mood to deal with."

I shook my head as we made our way back to her place.

I pulled into her driveway and turned off the car.

She looked at me then, her mouth parted ever so slightly, her eyes full of anticipation, the same emotion I knew she'd see in mine.

"Do you want to come in for a drink?" she asked, her voice as strong and steady as the Paris that I knew.

"If I go in for a drink, Paris, I'm not going to take a sip. You know that, right?"

"Then you'd better get inside."

And then she was out of the car, and I was doing my best to get out of my seatbelt to chase after her.

My pulse raced, and my hands practically shook, but then we were inside, and my hands were on her face, and my mouth was crushed to hers.

She tasted of the wine from dinner and our dessert—a little bit of coffee, and a whole lot of sweetness.

I wanted more. I craved it. So, I kept kissing, kept wanting more.

Our tongues clashed, her hands on my back, mine going over her shoulders and then down her back, cupping her ass over the softness of her dress. I rocked against her, my cock hard behind the zipper of my pants. I ached.

I pulled away, just enough so I could breathe in her scent.

"Are you sure, Paris?" I asked, my body shaking.

"Are you sure that I want you to kiss me and fuck me right now? Yes, I'm sure."

I grinned and then bit her lip gently.

"I like that word out of your mouth. *Fuck.*"

"Bite me again, and see what I do."

I bit her again, and when she moaned, I licked away the sting. Then she slid her hand between us, cupping my dick. I groaned, rocking into her hold.

"Can't wait to see what you've been hiding under those slacks of yours this entire time."

"You've seen me in jeans, too. I think they showcase my ass better."

"I might've noticed."

I licked up her neck and bit her earlobe.

"Oh?"

"Exactly. Now, no more talking. Get down to the fucking."

"That I can do," I said, and then I kissed her again, this time sliding my hand over the slit on her dress. I cupped her thigh, and then angled around, sliding up to cup her ass.

"What are you wearing under this?" I asked, my voice throaty.

"Why don't you check and see?"

I kissed her again, hard and fast, startling us both, and then I dropped to my knees. She gasped when I slid her dress up her thighs and breathed in her scent, licking my lips at the sight of her in a very tiny green thong.

"Look at you all matching."

"The dress didn't work with a bra, though, so that's about it," she said, running her hands through my hair.

"Well, then," I said, trying to sound casual.

I was anything but casual.

I licked up her leg, nibbling gently on her inner thigh, and she started to shake. I pulled away, looking around.

"I'm going to get you on the table."

Her eyes widened, and then I lifted her up as I stood. She wrapped her legs around my waist.

She crushed her mouth to mine, and I moaned this time, doing my best not to drop her as I made my way to her dining room table. I set her on the edge, then went back down to my knees.

"My table's pretty sturdy, but I don't want to break it."

"Then you better hang on, princess."

"I'm not your princess."

"No, you're my Paris, at least for the night. So, let me taste."

And then I shoved her panties to the side and licked. She gripped the edge of the table, her legs over my shoulders as she moaned my name. I'd never thought hearing her moan my name would hit me as hard as it did, but I almost came right there in my pants, fully dressed, and she hadn't even touched my dick yet.

Jesus Christ.

I kept going, licking and sucking and teasing her outer lips with my fingers. And when I parted her folds and gently probed her, she moaned, her inner walls clamping around my finger tightly. I gently worked in and out of her, with one finger and then two, then three. I curled my digits, finding that special spot inside as my thumb worked her clit, as I blew air on her. And when she came, her whole body shook, and I lapped at her juices, wanting more, needing more.

I got to my feet and tugged up her dress. When the sound of fabric tearing hit my ears, I froze.

She looked at me then, with her eyes wide, full of passion and surprise, and I cursed.

"I'm so sorry."

"I don't care. I never need to wear it again. Get it off me."

"If you're sure." I pulled at the dress again, ripping it even more, and then suddenly she was naked on the table except for her heels, her panties only torn fabric on the side of her, the rest of her green dress in tatters around her. I couldn't help but look at her.

Her breasts were full, her nipples dark and hard, and she kept touching them, plucking at them as she molded the mounds with her hands. Her hips flared out just enough for my hands to grip, which I knew I would want to use when I took her from behind.

And while she was splayed out in front of me, one leg wrapped around my hip, the other dangling, I knew I couldn't wait much longer.

I reached into my pocket, pulled out a condom, and licked my lips.

"Are you ready?

"Past."

I swallowed hard and then slowly unbuttoned one fastener at a time until I could slide off my shirt.

Then I undid the button on my pants and lowered my zipper before pulling my boxer briefs down past my butt. I didn't bother taking off my shoes or entirely removing my pants.

My cock sprang free, hard and ready to burst at just the sight of her, the taste of her.

And when I slid the condom down my length, I swore I saw her glisten even more at the sight.

I moved forward, bracing myself above her as I slid my cock between her folds, rubbing along her clit. I hovered over her more so I could kiss her.

Her hands moved down my back, and I knew she

would leave marks from her nails. I didn't care. I kissed her, hard and fast, our tongues tangling as we both fought for breath and control. My hands were on her hips, and then her breasts, and then on her.

When I pulled back, I swallowed hard and moved to take both of her wrists in one hand. I positioned her arms above her head, my cock still playing between her folds, then narrowed my eyes at her.

"Hands up here, beautiful."

"Are you telling me what to do now?"

"You want my cock? You listen to me."

"And then do I get to tell you everything that you did wrong at the end?"

"If you can find anything, baby. You're welcome to try. Let's see if you can even remember your own name by the end of it." And then I gripped her hips and thrust into her in one quick, deep movement.

We both froze, her inner walls clutching around me. I practically came again. However, she was the one who orgasmed. Her whole body shook, but she kept those fucking arms above her head as I'd instructed.

I was going to die right here, and I'd be one happy man.

I slowly slid out of her and then pounded into her again. She wrapped her other leg around me, and I thrust into her once more, pistoning hard one beat after another, both of us arching for each other. And then I moved one arm down to wrap around her back to pull her forward.

"Wrap your arms around me," I ordered. And she did, holding me close as I fucked her off the edge of the table. Both of us were panting, teeth and nails and lips and tongues. It was all one big moment of truth and ecstasy and...everything.

And when she came again, her pussy clamping around my cock, I came, too, her name on my lips as I crushed my mouth to hers, needing her taste. Needing everything.

As I stood there after, partially clothed, my cock still deep inside the woman I knew I was falling for, I knew I was in deep shit.

And I didn't fucking care.

Because this had been the best sex of my life.

The best *date* of my life.

And it was with the one person I was afraid would walk away.

Now I needed to figure out how to make sure that never happened.

Chapter 13

Paris

"You're serious? You did not do track."

"I did for a whole semester." Prior leaned back in his chair, grinning.

Our dinner plates were long gone, the tartlet between us nearly finished, and I smiled at him, shaking my head.

Tonight was our fifth date or so, although I didn't know exactly what we were counting anymore considering we still talked nearly every night, and worked together.

Apparently, going on a date with someone who was not your blind date but who had been there for the worst of them was life changing. Or rather just...changing.

"So, only a semester?" I asked, pushing away thoughts that were a little too serious for the time being.

"I got bored."

I put my hand over my mouth because I laughed a little too loudly, and people were starting to stare. I smiled from behind my hands, leaning forward.

"It's true. I got bored." He paused. "And there was this girl."

I rolled my eyes and took a sip of my water as I moved back. "Of course, there was a girl. There is always a girl, Prior."

"Which girls were you dating in high school?"

I scrunched up my nose and stuck out my tongue at him. Very mature. "I didn't date a girl until college like we both already talked about. Although I did realize that I liked boobs in high school, though I didn't realize what that meant at the time."

"I realized I liked boobs a little before that," Prior said, completely serious, even though his eyes were dancing.

"Why did you quit track?"

"Because I got bored for real. I run now because Nate drags me out, but I'd rather do anything *but* running to work out."

I raised a brow at him and gave him a pointed look. He coughed into his hand, and I swore he was blushing.

"Well, that is my favorite form of workout, but I was

talking about sports. You know us Bradys, we constantly want to play something, and that's how I get my workout in. But running a long-distance or even in a circle? I get bored. Nate was damn good at it, so I let him have it."

"And you didn't want to lose to your baby brother?" I asked, teasing.

He shook his head. "No, that probably would have annoyed me eventually because he was that good. Macon and Cross were already better at sports than I was, though, so I was probably used to it by then."

"Got to love sibling rivalry." I said it lightly, but my chest ached at the thought. I must have let something slip on my face because Prior gave me a weird look.

"What's wrong? What did I say?"

"You didn't say anything." I let out a breath. "I was just thinking of siblings. I used to have a sister, which is a bizarre way to put it. I had a sister. I still have her. Though she's no longer here."

Why couldn't I say the word *dead*? I should be able to do that. It had been long enough. I'd even said the word before when it came to her.

"Paris," Prior whispered, pulling me out of my thoughts. He reached across the table and slid his fingers through mine, rubbing his thumb over the space between my thumb and my forefinger. I looked down at our clasped hands and let out a breath.

The two of us were very good at not putting labels on our relationship, but this wasn't a first date, it wasn't even our second. And Prior was a friend.

He had seen me at my worst, when I had been bleeding and in pain and calling out for help.

Maybe he deserved to see some of my nightmares.

Because if tonight was the night that he slept over for the full night, then he might see a nightmare in truth.

We'd only slept together that first time, our other dates ending either with our group of friends, or us going our separate ways after some heavy petting. Neither of us had ventured into the next step of what our relationship could be. Even if using the word *relationship* was kind of scary.

Tonight, though...tonight I wanted to tell him. And then we would see where things ended up.

"How about we get the check, and you take me home, and we can talk?"

"Anything you want, I'm here. I promise." He gave my hand a squeeze before looking over my shoulder where the waiter presumably was. He smiled, did some gesturing thing, and soon, the check was there, and we were ready to go.

We were quiet in the car, and I felt like I had possibly ruined the mood, but I wanted to tell him. I hated that I had this secret that didn't need to be something between us.

We got into the house, and I went straight to my kitchen, contemplating hard liquor or coffee. I settled that argument by pulling out Baileys and starting the coffee maker.

Prior stood by my side for a moment before helping me with the coffee, neither of us having to say a word. He had made coffee in my home before, and I had made coffee in his, and it felt like this was another step.

How had this happened so quickly?

Or maybe it wasn't quick at all.

After all, it had been months since I had first realized my attraction to him, and over a month of us being together as we were now.

Maybe this wasn't as quick as my mind wanted it to be.

We settled on the couch, two coffees with Irish cream in our hands, and I let the warmth seep into my hands, my body cold.

"We can watch a movie. You don't have to say anything."

"I think I do. Because I feel like I'm keeping something from you, and I don't like that. I don't like hiding."

"You never hide. You're always the exact Paris you want to be."

I frowned. "What do you mean by that?"

Prior took a sip of his coffee, winced at the heat, then set it down on the coffee table.

"What I mean is that you are strength personified. You are brilliant, beautiful, and compassionate."

My heart filled, and I had no idea where he was going with this. "I wasn't asking for compliments, Prior."

"I know. You never would. You do what you need to do to get things done. What I meant by being the person you need to be is that nobody needs to know every aspect of you at work. Many of those people will never be your friends. They'll never be my friends. And we both understand that. It's like how some people have work personas. Sometimes it changes who they are completely, but never with you. You are who you are, but you put out so much strength, that sometimes people can't see beneath the layers. And I understand that. Especially with Benji around."

"Don't bring up his name in my house. I don't want to even think about him."

He hadn't changed much since the last time he blew out of my office, but he also hadn't outright accused me of anything recently either. I didn't know if that was because I had threatened him, or if he waited to threaten me again. Perhaps he'd figured out that Prior and I were friends at least and didn't want to upset a man he admired. I didn't know, I didn't really care, but I didn't mind the reprieve either.

I let out a breath, needing to continue, but not sure how.

"You don't have to say anything. We can just make out if you want."

I burst out laughing, shaking my head. Then his lips were on mine, soft. I sank into him, needing his embrace.

The mug was still between us, so he pulled back, taking it from my hands and setting it on the table.

"Talk to me, Paris."

"Her name was Tracey. She was so beautiful. We were both born blond, and my hair eventually darkened to what it is now. I don't know what her hair would have turned into. I think it would have darkened like mine, but hers was always a little lighter than mine. Mine was a little more like corn silk. At least that's what my grandma said once when we were little. Before she died, anyway."

I could still remember my grandma saying that before she lit up her cigarette and walked away to go pour another glass of cheap whiskey.

Grandma had been nice, a drunk, but she never hit me.

Not like the others had.

"My parents were not good people. They drank. They did whatever drugs they felt like. I don't know why they chose to become parents. In all honesty, even though my mom always said that we were planned because she wanted to have kids in her sober times, I didn't believe it."

"Paris." Prior let out a breath. "No, I don't want to interrupt. There's nothing for me to say."

"I've always heard the way you guys talk about your parents, how they're not here now but were always there before. And they constantly visit."

"You met them, right?"

I nodded. "When Macon and Cross were in the hospital. Yes. I didn't get to talk to them, but I met them in passing. They love you so much."

"They do. And eventually, I think they'll move back to be with their grandbabies when they come, but they love us."

"I don't think my parents loved me. Or Tracey. I think they wanted us because it was what you were supposed to do. Either that or my mom wanted to keep my dad with her. That's why I think she had Tracey. And I think I was an accident and am why they got together in the first place." I let out a breath. "It doesn't matter. But I had Tracey. She used to sing. She had such a beautiful voice, like a little angel's. When Mom and Dad started fighting and would slap at each other and hit and scream, she would come into my room, and we'd hide under my covers. When we moved to the trailer and we had to share a room, she slept in my bed, and we held each other close. Even as we got older, we always had each other because we knew we weren't going to have them."

I let out a breath, the memories coming back so quickly I could taste them—the stench of whiskey on their breath, the feel of hands on skin when they pounded into flesh. I could still hear the air conditioner running on its last leg, the trailer shaking when the wind got to be too much.

"My parents started hitting me long before I can even remember. A swat on the butt here or there. And then when I got old enough to try and duck away, Dad hit harder. And Mom would help. He would hit and slap and use his belt. If dinner wasn't served on time, or if we didn't do what we were supposed to do, even if they hadn't told us what they wanted. Then, sometimes, they got drunk and started having sex right there in the living room after fighting. And if one of us made a noise from our bedroom, crying or trying to do our homework, they would stop whatever they were doing, get dressed, and come and hit us because we interrupted what they were doing. When Mom stole Dad's drugs once, he blamed it on me, and hit me so hard I broke my cheekbone. Child services came, but they lied and said that I had fallen off my bike."

My hands were shaking, and when Prior reached out to hold them, I didn't back away.

"I didn't have a bike, Prior. I never did. We didn't have that kind of money. And even if we did, it would have gone for drugs anyway."

Prior didn't say anything, he simply held my hands, rubbing his thumbs over my skin as I kept going.

"My parents always kept jobs, that was the one thing they were good at. It was only for drugs. And booze. Or whatever else they could get their hands on. They would have orgies in our trailer and bring over whoever they wanted to fuck and do whatever they wanted. They wanted to live a life that meant having fun, gluttony and everything they could possibly have. Somehow, they had kids in the middle of it. And when Dad got too angry, he would hit me, over and over again. And then Mom would join in. Sometimes, Mom would hold me down while he hit me harder and harder."

"Baby."

"I know. I'm fine. They only broke a couple of bones. They got good at that. They didn't want child services to come. They didn't want to go to jail." I took another breath before continuing.

"Then they went after Tracey."

"Jesus," he whispered.

"Pretty much. When Tracey got old enough, Daddy started hitting her, too. And when I tried to protect her, he hit me harder. And then Mom would hold me back, so he could keep going at Tracey." I shook my head at Prior's questioning look. "They never touched us like that. Ever. That wasn't something on their radar. Although a couple of the guests of my parents' orgies gave us weird looks, Mom protected us from that." I let out a rough chuckle. "At least, she tried. Then she distracted them and pretty much had whoever she wanted on the couch and in her bed. One night, though, it was my birthday, and I came home from school with a present. It was a little candy bracelet, something that a friend gave me. It was so cheap that the candy probably would have made me sick if I'd had a chance to eat it."

After a minute, I didn't say anything, and Prior leaned forward and brushed my hair from my face. I leaned into his touch, inhaling his scent, and just...breathing.

I wasn't back in that trailer. I could do this.

"Dad called me a whore, snapped the candy right off my wrist, and then hit me with it. And then he choked me before he kept hitting and hitting and hitting."

Tracey was there, and she was so sad because it was my birthday, and they usually never hit me on my birthday. It was a weird thing, but it was like a present not to be hurt. I almost forgot about that, but they never did that." I shook my head when he opened his mouth to speak. There wasn't anything to say. "Daddy looked up, so furious that Tracey would say anything, and he back-handed her so hard she cracked her head on the cheap Formica counter and fell to the ground. There was blood everywhere, all over the floor, all over the wall, all over me. She wasn't dead, not yet. She was still moaning, and Mom was screaming, thrashing Tracey's shoulders down to the ground, screaming that she wanted her to wake up. It was only making it worse. And then Daddy hit me again, so hard that I didn't wake up for a minute or two, and then I came to and heard crying, and I thought it was Tracey, her little voice. But it was only in my dreams. They were holding her body, blood covering them both, and she was dead."

Tears were streaming down my cheeks, and I hadn't even realized it. Prior picked me up, the strength in his arms surprising me, and then I was on his lap, and he was holding me, sliding his hands down my back and through my hair, just holding me.

When was the last time I had been held like this when thinking those thoughts? My friends had done it, but a man had never held me like this.

And I didn't know what to make of it.

"Apparently, we had made enough noise that the neighbors in the trailer next door called the cops. They gave Dad manslaughter, Mom a lesser charge. They leveled them both with a bunch of other charges that I don't even want to get into, but it was enough that they were in jail for a long time. Somehow, though, enough time has passed. They both got out. So, when you and I were at that Greek Mediterranean place? That was the call from the detective, saying that Dad had gotten out."

"He's out right now?" The anger in Prior's voice calmed me somehow.

"Yes, Mom's been out for a couple of years now. They're not here. The detective said that they're keeping an eye on everything and will let me know if anything changes. I'm still afraid he's going to show up one day, though, you know? Or Mom will. But mostly Dad because he's the one who hit me the most. Mom just let it happen."

"And you think the attack..." he asked, not even finishing his sentence.

I shrugged. "I told the local police about it. And they got in contact with the old detective on the case. We don't know. There's no evidence, even though I fought back. So, they're still trying to figure out who it could have been. Because both of my parents, if I even want to use that term, have alibis."

"I don't know what to say. Other than, I'm sorry. And I want to hurt them for daring to touch you, and for taking such a light from this world. I also don't want to get too violent and scary."

"I want to murder them. Slowly. I want to hear their screams. I want them to pay for an eternity for what they've done. So, you getting violent with them? That's not going to trigger me. It might trigger other people, but for me? I just get angry. So, we can both dream of different ways to end my parents for what they did to Tracey. There's nothing else I can do right now."

"And what they did to you, baby. I could hurt them for that alone."

"You're right. I just...anyway, that's my big secret. And I have nightmares sometimes, and I see a therapist. And I'm trying to deal with it, but sometimes I wake up, and I scream, and I thrash out. And it sucks."

"That time you had a mark on your neck at work?"

"I didn't even know you saw that," I said, my eyes wide.

"I noticed a lot of things about you Paris. Probably before I should have."

He shrugged, and I blushed.

"That was a dream. I woke up screaming, but I got through it. If you ever spend the night here, you're going to have to deal with the fact that I might wake up screaming.

"I'm going to stay the night tonight if you'll let me," he said, his voice low. "I'm just going to hold you. I think that's what we both need, nothing else, but I'm going to hold you. And then if you wake up, I'll still hold you. To be honest, I have nightmares about Arden dying, about me not being able to do anything for her when she gets flare-ups. I have nightmares about seeing both my brothers in the hospital. I have stress dreams where I can't finish my homework for classes I didn't realize I was taking," he added, and I laughed. "I have a lot of nightmares, and sometimes, I talk in my sleep when I'm stressed out. I don't sleep with women often." He frowned. "I have sex, but I don't sleep over, and they don't sleep over usually."

"Tonight?" I asked.

"Tonight...tonight, I'm going to hold you."

And he did. We finished our cooling coffee and then got ready for bed, him in his boxers, me in an old T-shirt and shorts, the least sexy thing I owned. I leaned into him, falling asleep to the sound of his heartbeat beneath my ear.

I didn't have a nightmare.

And when we woke up, his mouth was on mine. And then he was inside me, both of us arching into each other —a breath, a touch. Making love.

I was falling for Prior Brady, and I didn't even know when I had begun to fall. Regardless, I knew I was going to land soon.

And as I gasped, both of us coming together, I wasn't sure if it would hurt when I completed that fall.

Chapter 14

Paris

I LEANED AGAINST THE DOORWAY, MY ARMS FOLDED over my chest, a brow raised. "So, it's your last day."

Prior grinned at me, his eyes brightening. "Finally, right? I mean, there's only so much I can take," he said deadpan, and I resisted the urge to flip him off.

After all, we were at work, and being crude wouldn't be a great thing. As it was, we were good about not even flirting or touching while at the office, and though we were dating, nobody needed to know that. It might not be against the rules, but it still wasn't good to flaunt our relationship or skirt the lines of what constituted appropriate workplace conduct. We could wait until later to be inappropriate with each other.

I smiled, my heart doing that annoying pitter-patter thing when I looked into his eyes. I wasn't sure what that was about, but I needed it to stop, thank you very much. "Anyway, I finished up the last bit of our project today, at least my part. I'm sure your replacement's going to have to go over everything you've done and change everything because, dear God, you do need some help."

Prior rolled his eyes. "Sure. Whatever you say. I mean, you were the one who oversaw everything and double-checked, so I guess you'd be the one in the wrong in the end."

"Oh, shush."

"I'm sure you wanted to say something a little more vulgar."

"Maybe. I did finish up the last part, signed, sealed and delivered back to your inbox."

"Great. I have a few more weeks on it probably, but I'll be at my old office getting things done."

"And the new hire should be here on Monday. *Finally.*"

We both knew that I was saying "finally" for many reasons. Mostly because while I enjoyed working with Prior—he was probably the best person I had ever worked with—I was also tired of having to hide my emotions when it came to him. Considering that I was still figuring out what those were, I would prefer not to add an odd deception into the mix.

"You're just going to let her talk to you like that?"

My shoulders tensed at the voice behind me, and Prior's jaw clenched. Prior spoke first, thankfully, because I wanted to scream. "We were kidding, Benji. Get back to your desk."

"You're not the boss of me. What the hell is with you two? I knew you guys were fucking, but I didn't realize you guys were going to fuck all of us over."

I rolled on him. "What on earth do you mean?"

"About you guys fucking? Everyone knows it. We're all talking about it."

I looked past him at the others on our floor, and they shifted from foot to foot, not looking at me.

Oh, so that's how it was. Maybe I needed to leave and get a new job. This was too much.

"It's none of your business." Prior sounded calm and cool, but I knew he was anything but. He was as hot-headed as I was and had to force himself to hold it back like I was trying to do.

"Seriously, Benji, just walk it off. Don't say something you're going to regret," Prior added.

"Look at you, a team. Is this how you got to where you are in your business?" Benji asked me. "Fucking your way to the top. I guess you're a decent piece of ass, but you're lucky that your little boyfriend will be gone. You're going to be following right on his heels. After all, I already told George what you've been up to."

My hand shook at my side, and I could feel Prior coming up behind me. I held up my hand, hoping that he would see that I could handle this. And I was going to handle it.

"I'm done." My voice sounded calm to my ears, but anyone who knew me would be able to hear the rage.

"You're finally going to quit?" Benji asked, his eyes gleaming with a manic anger I didn't understand. He'd had an alibi for the time I'd gotten attacked, but maybe it was a lie? Because that same sense of dread filled me when I looked at him, and my mouth went dry. I ignored all that and focused on what I needed to say.

"I'm done taking this. I only did for this long because I thought if I ignored you, you would go away. But that hasn't been the case. What you said right now? It was beyond inappropriate. I could sue you for your words alone. And everyone else on this floor, even if they won't stand up for me, heard it."

"We did," Susan, one of the only women on my floor said.

"We did," Trevor added. Warmth filled me, but I ignored it because I needed to focus on the horrible person in front of me.

Benji scoffed. "So what? George loves me. We golf every weekend. I'm the one getting ahead in this company. Your little boyfriend or fuck buddy or whatever the hell he is, is leaving."

"I'm headed for a promotion, in fact. I'm not even going to be attached to this branch. So, we were never in a competition."

"Oh, fuck you, too. In case you haven't gotten enough fucking from her."

I opened my mouth to say something and noticed that both Trevor and Susan had their phones out, recording everything.

Well, they were going to stand up for me, and I would finally have proof of Benji's bullshit. I was tired of this. And if George didn't take what I had to say seriously? I might sue. Regardless, I was leaving. I'd find a new job. Work, even if I loved it, was not worth *this*.

"I don't know what you have against me, but this is cruel and beyond horrible. I do not have to take this anymore. And you can stop. You can walk away nicely, and I won't sue you right this very moment."

"Big words for a big bitch."

Prior was there right behind me, but I stood in front of him, blocking his way.

"Don't hurt him, he wants to sue you."

"I don't think the lawsuit will be from Benji," a voice

said from the elevator. I froze before I slowly turned to see our boss, George Haberman, walking towards us.

I did not like George. He was part of the good old boys' club, someone who had gotten this job because of his family and rarely worked. However, he usually let us do what we needed to do and made sure we had amazing projects that utilized my talent and fulfilled my mind.

I hoped to hell he would be on my side about this.

Benji puffed up like a peacock as though he hadn't heard our boss's words. "Hey, George, can you believe how she speaks to me? It's like I've been telling you."

"You've been telling me a lot of things about Paris. And Prior. And a few other people around here. Why don't you come with me to my office, Benji? We need to talk."

Benji looked nervous, his face going almost gray. "What do you mean? You can tell everybody about my upcoming promotion right here."

Promotion? This was the first I'd heard of it.

"The papers weren't signed, Benji. And for that, I'm grateful. We can do this right here, though, if you want. You're fired. And, if we're lucky, Paris will only sue you and not the whole company. Those recording this, I would love a copy. Benji? Come with me."

Everybody started talking at once, and then Prior was there, holding my hand for a bare instant, giving it a squeeze before letting go. I blinked, not knowing what to say, not knowing what to do.

I had a feeling my work situation had just gotten a thousand times better.

In the end, though, I wanted to throw up.

By the time I got home, I was exhausted and sweaty but relieved. Benji would no longer be with the company. I would not be suing George and the corporation as of yet. There would be more paperwork and other things that I would need to figure out with regards to Benji. George had even helped, offered to assist me with getting a restraining order against Benji, but I didn't think that was necessary. Although Benji hated me for who knew what, reasons that I didn't understand, I didn't think he was the one who had attacked me.

The fact that I still didn't know who had, worried me. Honestly, I didn't think it was him.

Prior wasn't going to be at the office anymore, and I kind of hated the fact that the little cake the office had bought, and the little going away party and been marred. However, there wasn't anything we could do about that.

We would all still see Prior if he ever showed up again at the building to work on other projects, something he had said he wanted to do. And I would see him any day I could. Because somehow, our relationship had turned serious.

So serious that I thought maybe, if I let myself acknowledge it, I was falling in love with him.

He had let me fight for myself, even when he wanted to be the one who screamed and shouted and hit.

And maybe if we hadn't been at work, I would've let him.

I probably would've hit Benji as well, but that wouldn't have stopped anything.

Prior knew who I was and liked it. He saw my strengths and my weaknesses, and he didn't put me down because of them. He helped me elevate myself somehow.

I didn't know how that had happened, how I found myself wanting to be near him even when we had just seen each other. Yet here I was, thinking about him as I sat in my house and waited for him to show up. We weren't even going out on a date. We were going to make dinner together and watch a movie and probably make out and then go to bed.

Okay, and have sex. I wanted some hot, dirty, sweaty, kinky sex.

That's what I loved.

I thought maybe I *was* falling in love with him.

I still couldn't quite believe that I was sitting here on

my couch, waiting for...gasp...my boyfriend to come to my house so we could have an at-home date.

I had thought going on blind dates set up by my friends because of our pact would send me down a new path, and I had been right.

I honestly didn't think I would see Prior the way I was now if he hadn't been there for those last two horrific dates.

He had seen me at my most embarrassed, and my worst, and he hadn't left.

And that was everything.

I didn't know what would happen next with us or even with work now that Benji was gone. It felt like something had shifted, it had changed.

Maybe I could be happy.

My doorbell rang, and I grinned, thinking of exactly what Prior and I would get up to later. I had been relaxing and thinking so much that I hadn't started getting dinner ready. I liked messing with Prior near the fridge when we tried to figure out what we needed to make.

Knowing us, we'd end up simply making out and ordering in.

I wouldn't mind that either.

I opened the door without looking and froze.

Screams filled my mind, bile coated my tongue, and I

started shaking. My fingers dug into the wood of the door, and I forced myself to see the man in front of me.

He looked as if he'd aged at least thirty years, even though it hadn't been nearly that long. He had deep grooves near his eyes, deeper ones near his mouth from where he frowned, but no smile lines. He had gone bald on the sides, the rest of his hair now gray.

He'd gained weight in his belly, yet still looked the same somehow. Maybe a little weaker.

No, I was wrong.

He looked smaller. Was it because he'd aged? Because I knew his fists couldn't hurt me anymore? He was so different. He wasn't the man of my nightmares, and yet, he was. Standing here in the flesh, holding me captive.

"What the hell are you doing here?" I croaked out, surprised how I could even speak at all.

"I didn't know if I should call first."

"Are you kidding me? Get out of here. I'm going to call the police. You can't be here."

"I know. I know I'm not supposed to be here, and I won't be here for that long. I need to talk to you."

If he was here, that meant he had broken his parole, right? He wasn't allowed to be near me. Right? I couldn't even remember the rules. Maybe he had done this before. Had he been the one to attack me?

I started to shake and then went to close the door. I

looked at his face, at the evident sorrow there, and all I felt was pity. Pity and fear, and I wanted this to end.

A car pulled up behind mine, and Prior got out, confusion on his face. Then he narrowed his eyes and stormed towards us.

"Paris?"

"I'm okay. It's just Skeeter. My dad."

I didn't like calling him that. I had never mentioned my father's name before, so Prior wouldn't have known who I was talking about if I didn't elaborate.

He moved forward and stood between Skeeter and me.

I put my hands on Prior's back, catching my breath, his warmth seeping through my palms as I closed my eyes. I took in a deep breath, telling myself that I wasn't in the same place I had been before. I wasn't that little girl any longer. I wasn't going to get hurt today. I had stood up to Benji, and I would have stood up to my boss if I'd needed to.

I could stand up to the man who killed my baby sister.

"You need to back the fuck off. Get off this property. We're calling the cops right now."

"You have every right to call the cops and take me away. I just wanted to say I was sorry. Sorry for everything. Me telling you I'm a changed man isn't going to do anything for you. I didn't know how to write it down, I was never good with words. And I didn't want to call because I'm selfish. Or maybe because I was scared. You don't have to look at me again, Paris. You can stand behind your man, and I get that. Maybe I'd do the same if I had someone. I don't. And that's my fault, too. I'm sorry, Paris. I'm sorry for what I did to you. What I always did. I'm sorry for what I did to Tracey. I'm sorry that I lost her. I loved you guys."

"Shut up," I said and moved around Prior. Prior's jaw tightened. He didn't push me back. I stood next to him instead of in front of him. He was going to let me fight my own battles. I wasn't going to force him to watch me get hurt.

"Don't say her name. Don't talk about her. You need to go."

"Fair enough. I own all of it. You can do whatever you want to me. I'm going to burn in hell for what I did, and I understand that. I wanted to let you know that I'm sorry, though. And I'm not going to be here any longer."

"What are you talking about?" I asked, confused.

"Just want to let you know I'm not going to bother you anymore. No matter what. If I see you accidentally at a grocery store, I'll leave. I'll come nowhere near you, and I'll never hurt you again. I wanted to tell you I'm sorry."

"Fine. You're sorry. Now, go."

He looked at me again. This time, Prior had had enough. And I let him do what he needed to do.

"You're done. Go, before I do call the cops. You said your piece, she didn't have to listen to you. If I ever see you again, I will let out all the rage that I've been holding in today. And you do not want to deal with that."

"I understand, son. Take good care of her."

"I'll do a better job than you ever did," Prior said, and I saw the words hit my father like a slap. I didn't feel any joy in that, only pity.

My father gave me one last look and then walked away. I had a feeling this would be the last time I ever saw him.

He got into his old beat-up sedan and drove away, leaving me and Prior standing on my porch, my hands shaking.

And then Prior was in front of me, his hands on my face as he studied me.

"Baby?"

"Thank you," I whispered, and then I leaned into him, holding him close. I took in his scent, letting it soothe my nerves and breathed.

I had faced the man who had killed my sister, the man of my nightmares, and I had made it. I had said what I needed to, and I would never see him again.

As Prior held me, I thought of another thing that worried me.

Because the man who stood in front of me had not been big enough, had not been wide enough, had not been strong enough.

The man who was my father was not the person who had attacked me in the parking lot.

So who the hell had it been?

Chapter 15

Prior

I stood naked in my shower, my hand around my cock. I pumped it hard, the water turning lukewarm.

"Harder."

The voice in the shower with me felt like a purr against my skin.

"Any harder, and I'm going to squeeze myself blue," I said into the phone. I had my phone on the shelf where water couldn't get to it and was currently getting myself off while Paris did the same in her bed.

I had been listening to music in the shower when she called, and one thing had led to another. Now, my cock was in my hand, and I was ready to blow.

"What are you doing now?" I panted, barely able to breathe at this point.

"I have one hand on my breast, the other's playing with my clit. Will you help me? What would you do if you were here?"

"I'd be between your legs, licking you, one sexy lap at a time. Teasing your clit, using my hands to slowly tease you open, blowing cool air on that wet pussy of yours. Because you're always wet for me."

"Oh, I'm wet right now."

"Play with your clit and think of it as my tongue. I want to hear you come."

I had no idea how I was actually speaking or thinking right then because it was all I could do not to come immediately and fall in my shower.

"Prior!"

I could hear her coming, and that sent me over the edge. I shook, finishing myself off, and then I smiled.

"That's one way to wake up in the morning."

"It would have been better if it was your hand on me rather than mine. But we make do."

I smiled, thinking about what I was going to give her later that day. It had nothing to do with my dick.

Okay, maybe a little bit had to do with my dick.

"You headed over here soon?" I asked, wondering why I sounded so needy. Oh, right, because I was.

"I have a few things to do around the house, and then I'll be over. However, I will need something to eat. And not just your cock."

I barked out a laugh, even as I finished washing my hair in cold water.

"Oh?"

"Yes, I will eat your cock. First, however, I'm going to need food. And it's tough to hear you over the shower, so I'll see you soon."

"See you soon."

She ended the call, and I couldn't help but wonder why I had felt the urge to say something more after "see you soon."

I love you?

Right, that's what I wanted to say.

Hell.

I loved Paris.

Jesus Christ.

The water was only getting colder, so I rinsed out the product from my hair and turned off the water. I got out of the shower and grabbed my phone on the way.

I made sure that my phone was still dry, and then dried myself off, thinking about how quickly things had changed. And yet, maybe they hadn't.

I had been waiting for a serious relationship, even if I hadn't actively been looking for one. I had thought I had that with Allison. Only we were simply two people who occasionally saw each other and fucked once in a while. It was crude, not the nicest thing to say, but it was the truth.

We had never exchanged keys. We had never hung out just to...hang out. It always had to do with sex or her needing something from me.

I hadn't realized that until it was over. Now, it was a stark reminder that everything that I had with Paris was completely different.

I was no longer working at her branch of the company, so I didn't have to worry about any issues there. Things were going to get better for her at work now that Benji was gone. I didn't want to think about that and swallowed the anger that rose.

We were making inroads. And today, I was going to give her something that meant that.

I only hoped that she was responsive to it. Of course, now that I thought about it, it sounded like I was overreacting and making a big deal out of something that could be normal practice. Sensible.

Or too big of a step so quickly.

I got dressed and went to see what I could make her for brunch. She'd had a girls' night the night before, so she hadn't stayed the night as we had originally planned. She needed girls' time, and I understood that. So, I had hung out with the guys. Now, I was starving and couldn't wait to see her.

Times sure had changed.

I turned on my music again, dancing poorly throughout the kitchen as I figured out what I needed to make. I had a bottle of champagne for mimosas because she loved those—we were millennials, after all, it was what we were supposed to do.

I laughed at that, even if nobody else heard the joke, and then figured out what else I could make for her.

I liked cooking, even if I wasn't the best at it.

I enjoyed making sure that she was cared for because I knew not a lot of people had done that for her in the past. Her girls did it now for sure. And I would be forever grateful that she had found a family amidst the ruins of what she had grown up in and with.

My hands fisted on the counter, and I counted to ten, doing my best not to imagine hurting the man who had hurt her.

I couldn't change the past, but maybe I could make her a future promise.

I only hoped that she wanted the same thing.

I couldn't pinpoint the exact moment that things had changed for me, the time where I could say that, from this exact point, I loved her and wanted to see where we could go with our lives together. The feeling had been steadily building, and now I didn't want to turn away from it—something I might have done in the past.

Not with Paris.

That meant something.

The doorbell rang, and I frowned at the clock, wondering how she had gotten here so quickly. Maybe she hadn't done her hair. We were just going to have a lazy day. I wouldn't mind that.

I looked at all the vegetables and eggs I had on the counter and figured they could last for a minute while I went to the door. I walked over, wearing only gray sweatpants and nothing else since I hadn't bothered to finish getting ready yet. I opened the door, about to make a joke about my dick because...hello, it was Paris and me. Instead, I froze, blinking quickly and wondering if I should have perhaps looked through the peephole before I opened the door.

"Baby."

"What the fuck are you doing here?" I asked Allison as she tried to push her way past me.

She nearly stepped on my foot with her high heel, and I involuntarily took a step back. She put her hand on my chest, gliding past me into my house.

I couldn't physically stop her. If I did, then I'd have to put my hands on her, and I'd end up throwing her out on her ass.

And that wasn't something I was about to do.

"I asked you a question, Allison. And I didn't invite you in."

"I wanted to say I'm sorry."

"What do you mean? Wait, I know what you mean. Get out. You're not wanted here."

I saw the hurt mixed with calculation in her expression, and I wondered how I could have been so wrong about someone. Then again, I hadn't looked beyond the surface. Just as she hadn't. We had been who we needed to be for each other in the moment. We weren't anything more than that. We never had been. And it had taken me too long to realize that.

"You don't need to be cruel," she said, and that calculating gaze was back.

"You're right. I didn't need to snap. However, you did just force your way into my home. I would like for you to leave, now."

"Let me say my piece first."

"I don't need to hear it. You and your guy Tony can ride off into the sunset. What you did in my bed, the fact that I had to get a new fucking mattress and sheets? That's in the past now. I'm over it. I don't need to hash it out."

"You replaced the mattress that you and I made love on?"

"Okay, then. We've officially reached a new stage of

what the fuck. You fucked your ex or whatever he currently is on *my* bed. Not *our* bed, mine. I got a new mattress mostly because I needed a new one anyway, and you were the final straw."

"I don't understand why you're saying these words to me."

"I don't know who you are right now. Because you are not the Allison that I used to date. Maybe I wasn't looking hard enough, and for that, I am sorry. You really don't need to be here, though."

She looked around my home, kind of frowned at my kitchen counter and all the groceries out there so I could make brunch for Paris.

"You're going to make a meal for her? You never cooked for me."

"Okay, we're done. Get out."

"I hope you're happy with her. You'll never have with her what we could have had, though."

"You're right. I have an open and honest relationship with her, and I know she's never going to fuck her ex in my bed."

"You don't need to keep throwing that in my face."

"If you leave, then I won't have to."

Someone cleared their throat from behind me, and I closed my eyes and let out a breath.

I turned to see Paris standing there, champagne in one

hand, a bag of produce in the other. She was wearing jeans and a tank top, her hair piled on the top of her head, and she had indeed not finished it for the day. Because today was supposed to be our lazy day, one where we could just hang out and do nothing.

And now she was walking in on me shirtless in gray sweats, her favorite thing on me for some unknown reason, with my ex standing in my house, tears streaming down her cheeks. It was too fucking early in the morning for this.

"Oh, we didn't see you there," Allison purred.

"No, don't do that," Paris said, shaking her head.

"Excuse me?" Allison asked.

"You heard him, he told you to leave, and he was very polite about it. I spoke to you before this, and you were nice. You were not on whatever trip you're currently on. You don't need to resort to whatever you're doing right now. You are a stronger person than this. If you don't get the fuck out of his house right now, I'm going to be the one who hits you. Because he's not going to force you bodily out of the building, because he's nice like that. I'm the bitch."

I held back a smile because she looked so fucking hot saying that.

Yes, I was fucking in love with Paris.

"Don't you dare talk to me like that."

"Out," I said.

"Prior."

"Don't whine. That isn't you. I don't know what's up with you and Tony, and I'm sorry about that. I'm sorry that I wasn't a good enough boyfriend. Except you don't need to be here. We're never going to get back together. And you shouldn't be acting like this. You're better than this."

"I hate you," she snapped.

"Whatever you feel, that's your right."

Paris spoke up. "You don't hate him. You just hate yourself right now. What you should have done is cut him out of all the photos with you, burn them, and then get drunk and move on. You don't come to his house and act like this. This isn't you."

"You don't even *know* me," she snapped.

"We've all been you before," Paris said. "Any woman who's had a bad day and has lost it has had a moment where she wanted to act like this. Not many actually do it, though. Don't be this person. Just...leave."

"You two deserve each other," Allison snapped and then stormed out of the house, pushing past Paris on the way. Paris saved the champagne and raised a brow at me.

"I guess we do deserve each other," I said.

"She wasn't always that weird, right?" she asked, closing the door behind her.

I reached around her, locked the door, and then kissed her hard, taking the groceries and champagne from her. "No. She wasn't. You don't think something's wrong with her and Tony, do you?"

"She looked as if she'd had her heart broken, nothing else. I can go out and try to find out if you want," Paris said.

I shook my head. "No, I'm not worried. I don't like that she looked so sad, though."

"And she came here and saw you in your fucking gray sweatpants without any underwear, so your dick looks lickably good."

I barked out a laugh. "That's why you like me in these gray sweats?"

"It's a meme. We all like our men in gray sweatpants when they ride low."

"Wow. I just learned something new. And I'm never wearing gray sweatpants in front of anyone else again."

"You're damned right. I'm the only one who gets to see your VPL."

"How much time have you been spending on social media recently?" I asked, watching her sit herself down on the counter.

"I had a long week when I wasn't going into work, and I happened to read a lot of blogs and fan fiction. I can't help it."

"I guess I'm going to be wearing gray sweatpants for you often."

"That is what I like to hear," she said, and I leaned down to kiss her again.

"You think she's okay?" I asked, still worried about Allison.

"Okay, I'm not going to be angry that you kissed me and were thinking of her. We can continue this conversation if you want."

I winced. "I don't want to think that I hurt her in some way that made her act like this."

"No, she's just selfish, and she wants what she can't have. If she does it again, and we notice something, we can see if there's an underlying issue. Honestly, I think she was hurt and trying to get what she can't have anymore. And she can't have you."

"Damned straight."

"So, kiss me again and don't think of her."

I set down what I was working with for brunch, wrapped my arms around her, and kissed her hard, biting her lip, slowly nibbling down her neck.

"Just you."

"You'd better."

I kissed her again. Paused. "Nothing's in the oven."

"Really?"

"Really." And then my lips were on hers, and I was

slowly stripping her out of her tank top. She'd only worn a little cotton bra, one that barely held her breasts, so I pulled it over her head. Her breasts fell heavily into my palms. I sucked on her nipples, licking, biting. And she moaned, reaching behind the band on my sweatpants to grip my dick.

I was already hard, wet at the tip, and she rolled her thumb across the crease, slowly squeezing, running up and down my length. I tugged at her jeans, working them down. Suddenly, we were both naked in the kitchen, both of us laughing as we kissed and touched.

I lay her on my tile floor, slid my hands under her ass, and began to lick, blowing cool air on her clit, eating her out exactly like I had told her I would when we were on the phone together in the shower this morning.

She arched under me, her hands on her breasts. When she came, I sucked at her orgasm, lapping up her juices before crawling over her, kissing her again, and rolling us both so I was on my back, and she was over me.

"On me," I growled.

"It's about time," she whispered.

I reached for the condom that I had set out in the kitchen earlier in hopes this might happen and rolled it down my length. Then she sank down on me, her pussy clenching my cock. She rocked her hips, moving achingly slow on my dick, riding me until both of us were screaming and panting. I arched up into her, slamming into her hard, over and over again, her breasts bouncing as I did. And then she leaned forward, palms next to my head, kissing me hard. I reached up, gripped her breasts, molding the mounds, pinching the nipples, needing to touch her. I needed everything from her. I moved my hands back down to her ass, spreading her cheeks so I could thrust deeper, fucking her hard in my kitchen. We both shouted, our mouths on each other as we came.

I rolled to the side, my cock still deep inside her as I looked down at her. We grinned, both of us laughing.

"I thought I said you had to feed me first," she teased, her voice hoarse with pleasure.

"I didn't stick my dick in your mouth. So, technically, you haven't eaten dick."

"Should I make the joke that my pussy has, or have we reached a whole new level?"

We both laughed again, my dick twitching inside of her. I sank down, my forehead on her shoulder as I laughed. I never thought I could feel this bliss.

This was what love was. Awkward moments, kitchen floor sex, and laughing while you were still hard and deep inside the woman you loved.

And I fucking loved it.

We cleaned up, both of us taking quick showers separately because we were both starving. Then we drank mimosas and ate a decently done frittata in my living room, and I simply smiled at her, watching the way she moved.

"What is with you?" she asked, giving me a weird look.

I shook myself out of my reverie. "Just looking at you. You're pretty hot."

I wasn't ready to tell her that I loved her. I was barely getting used to the idea myself.

"You're pretty hot, too. Thank you for putting on the rest of your clothes, because you in jeans is just as hot as you in sweatpants. Though it takes more work for me to get to your dick, and I needed to eat real food first."

I choked out another laugh. "Thanks for that." I let out a breath, setting my plate and glass down on the table. "I have something to give you." She opened her mouth to say something, and I shook my head. "Nothing dirty. I promise. It's something I've wanted to talk to you about. If it's too quick, though, you can say something. And you can give it back, and we won't talk about it again. Only...I wanted to tell you."

She went sheet-white for a second, and I thought I had messed up.

Instead, she smiled and gave me a weird look.

"What are you doing, Prior?"

I reached into my jeans' pocket, and her eyes widened

for a minute. I was relieved I hadn't put the key in a box like I had originally planned. I'd thought a little present would work, but that would look way too much like a ring when neither of us was ready for that.

"I got you a key to my house," I said.

Her eyes widened even further.

"If it's too soon, you can tell me to forget it. I'm over at your house, you are over here enough that I figured...why not? We can figure out exactly what it means together over time. Still, you have a drawer here and a toothbrush, mostly because we are both practical, and carrying a bag in and out of the house every day is ridiculous. Anyway, I wanted you to have it."

Paris bit her lip, and I was afraid I had fucked up. Instead, she reached down for her purse and pulled out a little fabric bag.

"Here," she said, handing over the little cloth pouch.

I looked down at it, then loosened the little ribbon and laughed.

"I'll be damned," I said. "You wrapped yours."

"I've had it in my purse for three days, and I had no idea what to do with it. I'm glad you did it first because this was scary."

I grinned, cupped her face, and kissed her again. "Beyond scary. So, you get to do the next big thing. Whatever it is. I did my part. I'm exhausted."

Paris took the keys away, set them down near her purse on the table, and grinned. "Exhausted, are you? It looks like I'm going to have to take care of you, aren't I?"

From the gleam in her eye, I knew I was going to like this very much.

And when she slowly unzipped my zipper and licked her lips, I knew I had chosen well.

So. Fucking. Well.

Chapter 16

Paris

TEARS NEARLY FILLED MY EYES, MY HANDS SHAKING. "Yes, I've fallen in love with you. From the deepest part of my soul, down to the very essence of my being. I love you."

"Do you talk to all chocolate pastries this way? Or only the ones in your hand."

I freed one hand to flip Dakota off before staring lovingly at the pain au chocolat that she had made and brought over especially for me.

My precious. My beautiful precious.

"Now you sound like Gollum."

"Did I say precious out loud again?" I asked, staring

lovingly once more at the half-eaten pastry with the chocolate oozing out in exactly the right way.

"Yes, and you're one second away from petting the damn thing. I have more, you know. You just need to come to the café."

"That would require me to put on non-stretchy pants. And after I eat this, I don't think I'm going to be able to fit into my jeans."

"Your leggings are perfectly respectable for the café. Go forth and eat."

"I don't think I'm going to be able to. Because, dear God, this is so good. So amazing."

"Am I going to need to give you some space? Because you truly sound as if you're about to make sweet, sweet love to your pastry."

"And maybe I should. Sweet, sweet love." I leaned forward, pressed my lips to the sweet essence, and got down to it.

"I've never heard you moan like that. Maybe I should have asked Prior if you moan like that."

"Shut up. I'm eating." I licked my lips and sighed.

"You doing okay?" Dakota asked, laughing.

"I'm doing splendidly," I said, going to the kitchen so I could wash my face and my hands. It had gotten a little messy.

"I love that you can joke with me about pastries. That

was a little much," Dakota said, wiping tears from her face.

"It just tastes so marvelous. And yet, so simple."

"There is nothing simple about puff pastry. The amount of folding and butter it takes to make that perfectly? So the butter doesn't seep out into the oven and make smoke? It's not simple."

"I figured that out the hard way once. Prior and I were thinking about making croissants on our own, and then I remembered the last time I tried to cook with that much butter. I almost caught my kitchen on fire. So, we decided against it."

"Look at you two, baking together and making plans to bake together. It must be serious."

I looked over at my friend, trying to sort through my emotions. "I think it is. I have no idea how that happened."

"It happened because you two are great for each other. I'm only sorry we didn't think to set you up with him."

"I'm kind of glad that it worked out the way it did. I know that's weird. I think we needed to like each other as friends first, or at least as acquaintances before we went on a date. I don't think a blind date would have worked well for Prior and me."

"Considering that you grumbled at him the first time you met him? Probably not."

"I feel kind of bad about that."

"He grumbled right back. It was probably a form of flirting."

I laughed. "Probably."

"Anyway, it's nice to see the two of you together. Gives me hope."

I didn't know if I should move the subject to her. "For your blind date?"

Dakota shuddered. "Yes. Let's not talk about that."

"You're next, though."

"Maybe we'll take a break or skip over to Myra."

"We both know that's not how this works. I take it you don't want us fishing in the same pool that Hazel and I seem to be bathing in?"

"Let's not talk about that. I have a feeling that Myra and Nate have their own thing going on."

"I think they are acting weird, too. I thought that was just my mind playing tricks."

"I don't know. However, she's good about not looking at him."

"Maybe he offended her in some way."

"Maybe. Or perhaps I'm seeing things that aren't there because I do not want to go on a date. Ever."

"You were the one who helped us come up with this whole pact idea."

"You're right. Yet you tried to give up."

"After terrible blind dates. Truly disastrous ones."

"I want to apologize for the orgy again."

"We've already discussed that we don't know if it was going to be an actual orgy or only a threesome."

"True, true." She paused. "I don't want to do this whole dating thing," Dakota repeated, her voice soft.

"Okay," I said, leaning forward. "We don't need to. We can skip to Myra or quit it altogether. Don't get that tone in your voice, okay?"

Dakota gave me a soft smile and shook her head before her eyes brightened again. Then she smiled like normal.

"Joshua's off with his friends, and my lunch break is almost over. I have to get back to the café."

"I could have gone in there today, you know."

"I know. I needed to leave, needed to breathe, and I thought I'd see one of my best friends."

"Still, I'm the best of the best, right?" I asked.

"Sure, Paris. Whatever you say." She kissed my cheek, and then I walked her to the door, closing it behind her after she left.

I flipped the locks and then went back to my kitchen, cleaning up the mess from my pastry. Dakota didn't always have a lot of time off, and while we usually all met at her café when we could, she also liked to leave the place. Apparently, today meant a trip to my house.

I still wasn't quite sure how I'd gotten here. A lazy Sunday afternoon while getting all of my housework stuff done *and* getting prepared for the next day at work. Yet I wouldn't be doing it alone. Prior was on his way over, and he was even going to use his key to get into the house.

My boyfriend—yes, a title and label and everything— was coming over to my house, using his key to get inside, and we were going to make dinner, plan for the week, and probably fuck hard on my counter.

Or maybe the couch.

Or perhaps both places. But either way, we were going to fuck loudly, and I was excited about that.

And, honestly, it wasn't only fucking. We made love.

Something I had always giggled about and said that I was doing to pastries like earlier rather than someone I cared for.

Somebody I loved.

I loved Prior Brady.

Today, I was going to tell him.

Somehow, in this mess of who I was, this complicated array of finding a relationship, I had fallen in love with somebody.

And while I hoped to hell that he loved me too, I

would understand if he needed more time. Honestly, I didn't know what a respectable amount of time for someone to fall in love was. I had never done the math on it before, nor did I know if there was even any math to do.

Either way, I had to fess up to my feelings and hope that he didn't run away.

Or say: "*I care about you,*" or "*I like you,*" "*I respect you.*" Or…"*I need more time.*"

And hopefully, there wouldn't be a Prior-shaped hole in the door.

Most people probably would have been able to say those three words that meant so much in the heat of the moment.

Not me.

I needed time. I needed the perfect time. Well, perhaps not perfect. But enough time where I could work through what I needed to say and not have it come out in a garbled mess.

It was probably still going to come out that way. At least I had rehearsed some of it and had gone through and untangled as much of my feelings as possible.

I didn't want it to only be lust or infatuation. I didn't want it to be the excitement of having somebody I could rely on and see myself with.

I'd already been through so much with him, and I

didn't want to mess things up by moving to this next step too quickly.

We already had each other's keys. That meant something, didn't it?

And not just ease of access.

I winced, cleaned off my counter, sanitizing as much as I could and thinking about exactly what we had done on the kitchen floor the day before.

I hummed to myself, grinning.

I was pretty sure my knees were a bit bruised, and so was his back. But it had been worth it.

I could not wait to do it again. Maybe this time in a comfy bed. After all, I had memory foam, and it cradled my muscles and joints perfectly. It was probably better for us to have scorching, dirty sex there where we could protect ourselves so we could keep doing it again.

I laughed at myself, humming a tune as I went about cleaning the rest of the house, waiting for Prior to get here while enjoying my time alone.

The sound of glass breaking echoed in my ears, and I blinked, wondering if something had fallen. I'd cleaned out my vases, so maybe that was it. I didn't think so, though.

And then a shadow covered me, and a hand clamped over my mouth.

I screamed, thrashing. Arms became a vise around my

middle, the hand around my mouth tightening. I struggled, trying to get free. I couldn't. Whoever had me tightened their hold, pulling and tugging. I tried to scream, attempted to get away. They dragged me out of the kitchen and towards the living room. I kicked, moving around, trying to figure out who it was.

The man, at least it felt like a man, pushed me down to the floor, and I screamed.

And I looked up, recognizing the shape and the build and the clothes of the person who had attacked me in the parking lot.

"Why?" I asked, trying to crawl away.

Another person stepped out of the shadows and kicked me hard in the side. They were wearing high-heeled shoes with pointy toes, and I swore I felt something break. I groaned, trying to roll away. Then the woman was on her knees, punching me, slapping my face and pulling at my hair. The man was there too, kicking, his hands around my throat as he tried to strangle me. I pushed away, trying to save myself, trying to do something. Anything. They were so strong together, though.

There were two of them, and it didn't matter that they were older, the woman weaker than me, because I was outnumbered.

And then the man squeezed enough that my airway got blocked, and I thought I saw stars.

Then the woman backed away and slapped the man on the back of the head. He released me, and I gasped for breath, clutching at my throat, trying to breathe. The man took my hands and pinned them above my head, his whole body pinning me down.

"You bitch," the woman snarled, and then I got a good look at her, at her dry hair, her wide, manic eyes, and the snarl that was so familiar.

"Mom?" I asked, disbelieving.

"Don't you call me that, you whore. You're nothing. You were always a waste of space. And now look at you, thinking you're all high and mighty with your big house and your big fuck toy. You're nothing. You sent me to jail. Do you know what they do to people in jail? I didn't deserve to go there. Your daddy might have because he was a sick son of a bitch. I never did. I was a good mom. And you sent me there."

"You killed Tracey." I expected the slap. I didn't expect it to hurt as much as it did.

Blood filled my mouth, and I blinked, trying to focus again. My head had hit the floor hard when I fell, and the lack of oxygen for that moment hadn't helped.

"Don't you dare speak to me. You sent me to jail, and you did nothing. You paid for nothing. You have this perfect life, one that I should have had. But no, I had to have you and your little brat sister. Well, fuck you. You're finally going to get what you deserve. And Kenny here is going to make sure that happens."

"Anything you want, baby," Kenny said, breaking his gaze on me.

I shivered, bile rising in my throat.

"I got myself a new man. Your daddy ain't worth nothing. Never was. Kenny here? He did good for me. Always did. You remember him, honey, you met him when you were a little girl at our house."

"I remember her," Kenny said, and I froze, my body recoiling.

I remember Kenny. He had been one of the men who had watched Tracey and me when we were younger. And now, apparently, Mom was with him. And she was out of jail. It had been her. It had always been her.

"You've been watching me."

It wasn't a question, but my mother answered anyway. "Yes, we had to make sure we could get in. Make you pay. And they're going to blame your father. Because he's the one who got the worst charges. And now he's out of jail, and I can finally get what I want. Revenge."

Mom stood up, began to pace, stretching her arms. She was high on something or coming down. I wasn't sure which. I was going to die today. I knew it. I didn't have my phone on me. I didn't have a weapon. And both Mom and Kenny were stronger than me in this state.

I was going to die unless I could find a way out of this. Though I wasn't sure I could.

Mom walked towards the kitchen, pacing again before I could say anything. A key slid into the lock, and tears started to prick at my eyes. No, it couldn't be. Please. Not now.

The door opened, and Prior walked through, a smile on his face until he turned into the living room and saw the tableau in front of him.

Me on the floor, kicking and screaming, the man above me, pinning me down and ready to kill me.

He didn't see what was behind him.

And even as I screamed for him, "Prior, behind you," it wasn't enough. I wasn't fast enough.

The light above shone on the blade as it arced down towards Prior's back. He shouted, turned. It was too much.

My mother stood, that manic gleam in her eyes as she looked down at Prior as he fell to his knees, the knife in his back, blood pooling all around him.

I screamed again.

I didn't think anyone would hear me.

Because the only person who might have, was right in front of me, dying before my eyes.

And there was nothing I could do about it.

Chapter 17

Prior

I SUCKED IN A SHALLOW BREATH, TRYING TO FIGURE out what the hell had just happened. I didn't think I had time to even focus on that. I turned over, wincing at the pain lancing through my system. I was on my side, and then there was another tug on my back, and someone was screaming.

Was it me? No, I didn't think I was screaming. Who was making that noise?

Paris. Paris was hurt. I was hurt. Someone had stabbed me? No, that couldn't be. I'd just walked in the door, and now, everything hurt. Everything ached. I was warm, too warm, and then I was cold. What the fuck?

My body shook, and I did my best to keep moving, to figure out exactly what I was supposed to do. Only I wasn't moving. And I wasn't thinking.

And then I heard Paris's scream again, her shout. And I could think again. There was pain, fiery pain that burned every inch of me. I couldn't think clearly.

I rolled to my front again, my back aching, blood pooling around me. I looked up at the shadow above me. The older woman wasn't looking at me. No, she was looking at Paris.

Grinding my teeth through the pain, I moved to my hands and knees and slowly staggered to my feet, leaning against the wall for support. I knew I was leaving blood everywhere, and I didn't know what she had stabbed me with or even how deep the wound had gone. All I knew was that it hurt, and if I wasn't careful, I could bleed out here and die. Die without ever being able to fight back, not even knowing the name of the woman who had hurt me.

However, that didn't matter right now.

I had to make sure Paris was okay.

I staggered forward and threw myself on top of the man who was looming over Paris.

I grabbed his shoulders, rolling to my back and screaming.

I didn't think the knife, or whatever had stabbed me, was still there, thank God, but my wound was. And it hurt. Then, I didn't feel much because I was rolling around on the floor with whoever the fuck had been attacking Paris.

Paris screamed again, kicking out, and out of the corner of my eye, I saw her get to her feet and punch the woman in the face.

I frowned, trying to figure out what was happening. I felt like I was two steps behind.

And then the man in front of me had his arms around my neck, trying to strangle me. I moved out of the way, rolled, taking him with me, and then I punched. Punched and pounded and used my fists. I didn't know if it was enough, but I was bigger than he was. And probably stronger, even if I was in pain.

I had to focus. Had to get this right.

Paris had to be okay.

"Prior!" she yelled. I couldn't focus. Not again.

"You think he's going to save you?" the woman asked.

"Fuck you!" Paris yelled, and I pushed the man off me and then punched him one last time, this time hard enough that I was afraid I had broken my hand. I didn't care. With the amount of blood all around me, I wasn't sure I would make it past the living room to even notice a broken hand later.

That grim thought in mind, I staggered over the unconscious man under me and crawled towards Paris.

She knelt above the other woman, slapping and hitting, tears streaming down her face.

And then the woman was unconscious, as well. I reached out and tried to grab Paris's arm to hold her back.

"Paris."

She froze, then looked over at me, her eyes wide and her face drained of all color.

"Oh my God, Prior. Stay with me."

What was she talking about? I was with her. I was totally with her. Wasn't I?

Time passed, and then there was crying, tears seeping into my shoulder, and I was on my side, someone pressing something to my back, but I didn't know who or what. The two bodies around us weren't moving. Were they dead? Was I?

I didn't know. Then my head was in Paris's lap, and she was crying, speaking to me. I couldn't understand.

She simply held me, whispered my name.

And all I could think of was that I hadn't done much. She had protected herself, and all I had done was get hurt.

"You saved me," she whispered. "You saved me."

"You saved yourself."

At least that's what I thought I said. It came out as a garbled mess, and Paris tried harder. Her tears were salty on my face, or maybe that was the blood pooling in my mouth.

I wasn't a hundred percent sure anymore. Everything hurt.

I didn't want to die. I didn't want this to be the last time I saw Paris. I wanted to be able to say goodbye to the people that I loved. To tell her that I loved her.

I didn't think I was going to get that chance. The last thing I heard before I fell back asleep, at least I hoped it was sleep and not death, was a whisper.

It couldn't be true. I must've been imagining things. "Don't die. I love you, too."

And then there was nothing. Only darkness.

At least the pain had gone away.

Chapter 18

Paris

I PACED BACK AND FORTH IN THE WAITING ROOM, THE cut over my eye bandaged from where I had somehow hurt myself when I fell. I was bruised, sore, and would have trouble speaking for the next few days because of the bruises around my neck. But I was alive. All because of the man that I loved. The guy who I wasn't sure would survive.

Because, somehow, he had walked into a nightmare, *my* nightmare, and had almost died. Was still in danger.

I would never forgive myself if he didn't make it out of this. Fuck, I might not ever forgive myself as it was.

"Sit down," Macon growled, and I looked up at Prior's brother, startled.

"Did you just growl at me?" I asked.

"Now sit your fucking ass down."

"Don't curse at her."

Macon raised at brow at Dakota's tone.

"I'm sorry. How about you sit your pretty ass down?"

That made me snort, even as Dakota's eyes narrowed.

I did, however, sit my ass down in a chair. I gripped the edges of the seat, my hands shaking, practically in my own world as I fought for air.

I had already spoken with numerous doctors and nurses and the police. They had taken my statement and had questioned me for over an hour.

They'd been very apologetic, quite understanding, actually.

Now, they were gone, doing what they needed to do as they took my mother and her boyfriend away.

I would deal with the consequences of what had happened later. I would take care of the blood in my home, the shattered glass, the screams that still echoed in my mind.

I would handle all of it.

As long as the love of my life was okay.

"You didn't need to be so rude to her," Dakota snapped.

"She wasn't going to sit down until someone yelled at

her. And I'm a person who yells. Apparently, I'm good at it."

The two of them stared at each other before Dakota turned away and went back into the part of the waiting room that had the vending area. Nate and Joshua were there, going over what type of M&Ms they wanted because, apparently, there were peanut butter M&Ms in the machine.

I knew Dakota was worried because she didn't want her son here, not after everything that had happened in the past. She had wanted to be here for me and for Prior. I saw that Joshua was pale, scared, and looked like he didn't want to be away from his mother.

"How about I take you home?" Dakota said, echoing my thoughts.

"I want to know about Prior."

"They can call us, and they can tell us everything that's happening. You shouldn't be here, Joshy."

"I'm not a baby. I know people get hurt. Cross and Macon got hurt. They're okay. And Paris and Hazel got hurt too, and now they're better. People get hurt, and now they're all good. But I need to make sure that Prior's fine, too."

He raised his little chin, and tears slid down my cheeks. Hazel and Myra were on either side of me, gripping my hands, lightly because of the bruising, and I knew they were crying, too.

I looked towards Hazel, noticed the tears. As I turned to Myra, I was wrong. She wasn't crying. No, she was pale, and there was anger on her features. So much anger.

I was mad, too. I felt like I had so many emotions running through my body right then that I couldn't quite focus. Couldn't quite breathe.

Nate came back into our part of the room, his hands in his pockets as he sat down opposite us, his gaze on Myra. Myra turned away first. I couldn't focus. I was going to throw up if I wasn't careful. I just needed to make sure Prior was okay.

He couldn't die tonight. He couldn't.

"Our brother is going to be fine," Cross said from his chair on the other side of Hazel. He stood up, then came in front of me and knelt.

"How do you know that?" I asked, my fear seeping through my words. I knew I should watch what I said because Joshua was listening, and Dakota wouldn't forgive me for scaring him. But I couldn't hold back.

"I know that because Prior finally found his happiness. He's not going to leave it now."

"Life doesn't work that way. And we both know that."

"Maybe for others. Not for Prior. He sets his sights on what he wants, and he fights like hell for it. He always has. And he's going to fight for you. Going to fight for what you two have."

"It's a knife wound. It's not some fated tale of fighting through magic. This is actual analytical and surgical. It's not imaginary."

"You've got to believe in him, Paris. Belief in what Prior can do. Belief in the people who are working to save him. It's what we have right now."

"I hope you have enough of that for all of us, because I'm scared."

"Then we will all hope to hell and back that Prior remembers exactly what type of fighter he is," Arden said, her hand held tightly by her husband's.

Nearly the entire family was here, our group whole again except for the gaping hole that was Prior. His parents were on their way, a familiar flight because they had already been here once for the shooting. What would it be like for them to be able to visit when it wasn't under the fear of death and horror?

I got up again after Cross left and continued pacing. Macon didn't growl at me this time. I had a feeling it was because Dakota was glaring at him, and he had his hands full distracting Joshua.

My whole body ached. The more I moved, the better I felt. At least, that's what I told myself.

I counted off the tiles—one, two, three. And I kept

counting, kept working numbers in my head until finally, the doors opened, and I turned so quickly I almost fell. Nate was there, holding my elbows as the others came around me, holding my hands, holding each other.

"We're looking for the Brady family?" a man said from the doorway.

"That's us," Cross said.

I vaguely remembered someone saying that before when we were here for Cross and Macon.

How much of my friends' blood would be spilled before we got through the hell that kept coming at us?

Blood roared in my ears as the doctors came in, explaining what had happened. I couldn't focus on what they were saying. I could barely hear at all. When people started crying, relief evident on their faces, my knees buckled. Then I was in Nate's arms, Prior's brother holding me as I tried to rationalize what was happening.

"He's going to be okay, Paris. He's going to be just fine. So fine, in fact, if he hears that I held you like this, he's probably going to hurt me. So, buck up and get strong. Because as soon as Prior's healthy, he's going to kick my ass."

And then I was laughing and crying at the same time, my arms wrapped around his neck as the others began to speak, the doctor explaining more. I would listen soon. I would ask the others what had happened. But for now, I needed to breathe. And I needed to see the person that I loved.

Unfortunately, I couldn't see him until the next day. It had been a long night. He was finally in his own room, safe, and hopefully waking up soon.

The others had already seen him, but I said I'd wait.

Was it because I was still afraid? Maybe. Or perhaps I simply wanted every ounce of time I could get with him, and if that meant waiting for the others to get their fill, then I would do it. I was never leaving again.

He looked so pale, so big in that little bed. Maybe they used special beds in movies or on TV to fit those big actors. Prior looked far too large for that cot of his.

They had it somewhat inclined, and he didn't have a tube down his throat.

Somehow, the knife hadn't hit anything too critical. He'd sustained slices to his spleen, though, hence why he had nearly bled out and died. They had removed the organ and explained that he might be more susceptible to infection and disease now, but there were injections and vaccines he could take to supplement that.

In the end, it could have been his kidney, or his liver, or something even more vital.

Nothing else had been cut into, not that they could tell, and they'd quickly gotten the bleeding under control once they removed his spleen.

He would be in pain for a while, and it would take some time before he could walk and move and play football like he used to.

He had already spoken to the others and smiled, and then he had fallen asleep again, his body exhausted and trying to heal itself.

After saving me.

And now I was alone in the room with him, too afraid to touch him.

He looked so fragile. My big, strong Prior with the strong jaw and thick thighs and broad shoulders. And yet I had almost lost him. Right when I had just found him.

I reached out, wanting to grip his hand, yet so afraid I'd hurt him.

"I'm not made of glass, Paris, baby."

I startled, blinking, my hand dropping. "Prior." My voice cracked, and I quickly wiped tears from my face.

"Don't cry."

"I might just cry. You almost died."

"I'd say the phrase 'so did you', but then I'll get angry again, and I don't think I have the energy to be angry right now. That'll come later."

I sat up and moved forward, still not touching him.

"You can touch me, Paris. Please, do. I need you to be real. I kept having dreams that you were standing there, right near me, yet I couldn't touch. So I need you to be real."

Tears were freely falling down my face now, and I reached out and slid my hand into his. It was so warm, he felt so alive. And when he squeezed back, I let out a choking sob.

"I told you not to cry."

"And I told you to shut up."

I laughed as I said it, a watery one that echoed Prior's.

And then I leaned forward and brushed my lips against his.

"You're very lucky the nurse let me brush my teeth before you got here."

"I don't care. You could stink, and you could have horrible breath, and I wouldn't care."

"That needs to be a Hallmark card."

"Why are you so much better at words than me right now? You were unconscious, and yet I'm the one who can't think of anything to say."

"Maybe because I had a lot of time while I was unconscious to think about what I wanted to say to you."

"Is that true?"

"It sounds like a great line, doesn't it?"

"I love you," I said quickly, not wanting to hold back any longer. "I was going to tell you before this and was trying to figure out exactly what to say because I know it's fast. Yet it doesn't seem fast at all. I love you so much. And not only because you almost died for me. I just love you. I love the way you make me smile. I love how you look at me when I'm walking towards you. I love the way I know you're looking at me when I walk away." He laughed at that, and I grinned.

"I love how you helped me with my air filter, and that you're always making sure I'm fed. I love the way you were my best blind date that wasn't a blind date. I love the fact that you were there when I needed you, and I know you always will be. I love you, Prior. I love you with everything I am."

"Jesus, you just took the wind out of my sails."

I coughed. "What?"

I had this beautiful speech planned, and there you went, outdoing me. Such a Paris thing to do."

"Am I allowed to flip you off right now while you're in a hospital bed?"

"You can do whatever you want, Paris. You want to know why?"

"Why?"

"Because I love you. I love you so fucking much. I love the way you smile at me. The way I know you're checking out my ass when *I* walk away."

"That was my line."

"And yet, it works for both of us."

"True. You do have a beautiful ass. In jeans and in those gray sweatpants."

"I will wear them both for you constantly."

"Also, in suit pants."

"Noted."

"And naked."

He laughed then, and then winced. "Oh my God, I hurt you. I'm so sorry."

"No, but I need to stop moving. I'll be fine. They've got me drugged up."

"Too drugged up that you don't know what you're saying and you're going to forget what I'm saying?"

"No, just drugged up enough. I'm going to remember everything. This moment? I'll fucking remember it all forever. Now, where was I?"

"I believe you were at my ass."

"Maybe later. For now..." he began, and I laughed.

"We are not talking about ass play right now."

"You say the most romantic things. However, I'll continue."

"Whatever you say."

"I love you. I love that you make me crazy. That you make me think. That you make me so protective, and yet I know I don't need to be because you can take care of yourself. I love the fact that you trust me. And how we fit together so easily it's like we always should have been where we are now. I love you. I cannot wait to see who we both become. Because I know I'm better with you."

"Prior," I said, not knowing what else to say.

"See? I think you're better with words. I got a little nonsensical there. I'm going to blame the drugs."

And then I leaned forward and took his lips.

"You're never allowed to leave me."

"Where did that come from?" he asked, searching my face.

"Because you almost died."

"Cross said it was your mom?"

"I don't want to talk about her."

"You don't need to. Just tell me a little bit. I don't know everything. And I want to know what happened in the end."

"My mom waited until my dad got out of jail to blame me for everything that *she* did. She blamed me for sending her to jail, so she hooked up with a man who didn't care about hurting people. He liked it. I don't know what's going to happen to her. I know she's going back to jail. Same as her boyfriend. She orchestrated the whole thing. The attack before, the stalking of my house, the getting into my home. All of it. And, somehow, if we hadn't fought together without even knowing it, we would be dead right now because that's what she wanted. She wanted to end my life for ruining her life and sending her away."

"Well, fuck her. You're way stronger than anything she could have brought."

"Not me. We. *We* did this. And don't you ever leave me," I repeated. "Ever. Because I don't think I can do this without you."

"This?"

"Navigating your family, our group, and life in general. You're stuck with me, Prior. I'm sorry. That's just going to have to be how it is."

He grinned then, and as the nurses came into the room to check on him, I held his hand and knew I wasn't going to let go until I was forced to.

I had fallen in love with Prior Brady.

The one man I hadn't expected, and the one man I hoped would be my last first date. Ever.

Epilogue

Prior

My knee ached, but I'd get over it. Because right then, I had something better to do. I gripped Paris's thighs, my fingers digging in as I licked and sucked. I loved the way she writhed on my face.

"I'm close," Paris panted.

"Get closer," I growled against her pussy.

"Prior!"

I licked some more, and used two fingers to spear her, curling my digits just right while lapping up her juices. She came on my face, and before she could even quit shaking, I undid my belt, slid my pants down partway, and slammed into her, both of us still nearly fully clothed. We each froze at the sensation of her cunt clamping around my dick.

"Oh God," she whispered.

"That."

And then I moved. I thrust in and out of her, pistoning until both of us gripped at each other's shoulders, our mouths latched on to one another's, needing each other. And when I came, she came right with me, both of us shaking to the point where I was afraid we were going to fall. After all, we were leaning against the couch, and she was wearing very high heels and a dress that looked sexy as fuck.

One that she needed to keep wearing because we had to be out the door...about ten minutes ago.

I was still deep inside of her, looking around for something to clean us with.

"I thought you said you were just going to tie your shoe," Paris said, laughing, still keeping me inside.

"I'm not even wearing shoelaces," I said with a laugh and kissed her hard again. I pulled out of her, and both of us cleaned up, laughing and kissing as we did.

Paris had to get a new set of panties since I was pretty sure I had heard them rip when I pulled them to the side to eat her out. That wasn't the first time that had happened.

"Prior Brady. I'm running out of nice underwear."

"Maybe you shouldn't wear any."

"I am wearing a dress with a side slit. No one's going to be able to see my underwear, but I am not going commando around your brothers."

I frowned. "Good idea. Let's not do that."

"Yes. Let's not. Because you know they're going to know that we had sex before we got there."

"Most likely. That's sort of why we're going to be late. They're all going to know, especially with that very satisfied look on your face."

"I'm pretty sure that's your satisfied look."

"You're telling me you weren't satisfied?"

"Twice. You know that. And stop saying *satisfied*."

"How about fucked."

"Fine, but don't say that around Joshua. Dakota is getting cranky because we keep cursing around her kid."

"You're the one who cursed around him the last time, and then blamed it on me," I said with a laugh as we got into the car.

"Well, you made me mad."

"No, I didn't. You just didn't want to make Dakota mad. You want her to get angry at me."

"Maybe. You can handle it better than I can."

"We both know that's a lie," I said, shaking my head.

We were heading to Cross and Hazel's house, the

Brady family dinner, this time with all of us in attendance.

Dakota and Myra were coming, as well, although I had a feeling the girls weren't too excited about it.

Not that they weren't always welcome. But with two of the friends as part of the pact now paired off with the Bradys, I had a feeling that Dakota and Myra didn't like the odds with my other two brothers.

Not that I was touching any of that with a ten-foot pole, thank you very much.

"So, who do we think is going to get in a fight first? Myra and Nate? Or Dakota and Macon?" Paris asked, echoing my thoughts.

"You know what? I was just telling myself I wasn't going to touch on that subject."

"That's very smart."

"And, of course, we can always have a play fight and yell at each other so we're the ones at the center of attention rather than the awkward...whatever fucking tension the other four have."

"You know, you're right. And I hear make-up sex is pretty amazing."

I grinned. "Make-up sex?" I asked.

"It can get rough. A little angry. And I know that you always wanted to try that ass stuff you talked about doing when you were in the hospital."

A car screeched behind me, and a horn reminded me that I probably should get back on the road.

Even though Paris was holding onto the Oh Shit bar, she was still laughing her head off, and I shook my head.

"Number one, I cannot believe you brought up ass play while we're on our way to a family dinner. Number two, we may have to start a fight anyway, not only for the other four but because I want to try this whole make-up sex thing."

Paris was crying, she was laughing so hard, and I just shook my head and reached out to grip her hand.

"Love you, buttercup," I said.

"Buttercup?"

"Well, I was going to call you *baby*, but that sounded like something I always say. And then I was going to call you *fucking hot wench*, but that didn't make any sense."

"You can always call me Paris, you know," she said, rolling her eyes at me.

"Maybe. Prior and Paris? That's a mouthful."

"I guess we'll have to come up with better nicknames."

"Fine. Is this what our fight is going to be about?" I asked.

"You're only thinking about make-up sex."

"Maybe I am. Hell, I can't wait."

"I was kidding about the ass play," Paris said quickly.

"You say potato? I say poe-tah-toe."

"You say playing ass play. I say doing ass play."

"Okay, I guess we're going to have that fight, aren't we?" she said with a wink.

I leaned over while we were stopped at the light and kissed her hard, falling more in love with the woman that I'd thought would be my adversary but had become someone so much more. Somehow, I had found my purpose, my happiness with the woman who had started off as someone I thought hated me, and eventually turned into this person I would die for.

Neither of us had ever expected to be here, yet here we were. There was no going back, and that was just fine with me.

Because her nightmares were a thing of the past, even though her past was a thing of nightmares.

We were moving forward, the two of us and our group, knowing we had a future laid out before us. One we might not have been prepared for, one we might not have counted on, but it was ours. And I couldn't wait to see where Paris would take me.

Because as she grinned at me, I knew that, no matter what, from this moment on, everything would be a surprise.

A surprise I wouldn't be alone to experience.

Ever.

THE END

Next up in the PROMISE ME SERIES?
Macon and Dakota in FAR FROM DESTINED
For more information, go to www.CarrieAnnRyan.com

WANT TO READ A SPECIAL BONUS EPILOGUE FEATURING PRIOR & PARIS? CLICK HERE!

A Note from Carrie Ann Ryan

Thank you so much for reading **FROM THAT MOMENT.** I do hope if you liked this story, that you would please leave a review! Reviews help authors *and* readers.

The Brady Brothers and the Pact Sisters are so much fun. Just don't tell them that I've give them group names LOL.

I hope you enjoyed Paris and Prior. Their book wasn't easy to write, with Paris surprising me left and right, but I hope you fell for them as I have.

Up next? Macon and Dakota. And oh boy....

And in case you missed it, Arden and Liam might be familiar if you read Wrapped in Ink!

And if you're new to my books, you can start

anywhere within the my interconnected series and catch up! Each book is a stand alone, so jump around!

Don't miss out on the Montgomery Ink World!

- Montgomery Ink (The Denver Montgomerys)
- Montgomery Ink: Colorado Springs (The Colorado Springs Montgomery Cousins)
- Montgomery Ink: Boulder (The Boulder Montgomery Cousins)
- Gallagher Brothers (Jake's Brothers from Ink Enduring)
- Whiskey and Lies (Tabby's Brothers from Ink Exposed)
- Fractured Connections (Mace's sisters from Fallen Ink)
- Less Than (Dimitri's siblings from Restless Ink)
- Promise Me (Arden's siblings from Wrapped in Ink)
- On My Own (Dillon from the Fractured Connections series.)

If you want to make sure you know what's coming next from me, you can sign up for my newsletter at www. CarrieAnnRyan.com; follow me on twitter at @CarrieAnnRyan, or like my Facebook page. I also have a Facebook

Fan Club where we have trivia, chats, and other goodies. You guys are the reason I get to do what I do and I thank you.

Make sure you're signed up for my MAILING LIST so you can know when the next releases are available as well as find giveaways and FREE READS.

Happy Reading!

The Promise Me Series:

Book 1: Forever Only Once

Book 2: From That Moment

Book 3: Far From Destined

Book 4: From Our First

WANT TO READ A SPECIAL BONUS EPILOGUE FEATURING PRIOR & PARIS? CLICK HERE!

Want to keep up to date with the next Carrie Ann Ryan Release? Receive Text Alerts easily!

Text CARRIE to 210-741-8720

About the Author

Carrie Ann Ryan is the New York Times and USA Today bestselling author of contemporary, paranormal, and young adult romance. Her works include the Montgomery Ink, Redwood Pack, Fractured Connections, and Elements of Five series, which have sold over 3.0 million books worldwide. She started writing while in graduate school for her advanced degree in chemistry and hasn't stopped since. Carrie Ann has written over seventy-five novels and novellas with more in the works. When she's not losing herself in her emotional and action-packed worlds, she's reading as much as she can while wrangling her clowder of cats who have more followers than she does.

www.CarrieAnnRyan.com

Also from Carrie Ann Ryan

The Montgomery Ink: Boulder Series:

Book 1: Wrapped in Ink

Book 2: Sated in Ink

Book 3: Embraced in Ink

Book 4: Seduced in Ink

Book 4.5: Captured in Ink

The Montgomery Ink: Fort Collins Series:

Book 1: Inked Persuasion

Book 2: Inked Obsession

The Promise Me Series:

Book 1: Forever Only Once

Book 2: From That Moment

Book 3: Far From Destined

Book 7.3: Dropout
Book 7.5: Executive Ink
Book 8: Inked Memories
Book 8.5: Inked Nights
Book 8.7: Second Chance Ink

Montgomery Ink: Colorado Springs

Book 1: Fallen Ink
Book 2: Restless Ink
Book 2.5: Ashes to Ink
Book 3: Jagged Ink
Book 3.5: Ink by Numbers

The Gallagher Brothers Series:

Book 1: Love Restored
Book 2: Passion Restored
Book 3: Hope Restored

The Whiskey and Lies Series:

Book 1: Whiskey Secrets
Book 2: Whiskey Reveals
Book 3: Whiskey Undone

The Fractured Connections Series:

Book 1: Breaking Without You
Book 2: Shouldn't Have You

Book 3: Falling With You

Book 4: Taken With You

The Less Than Series:

Book 1: Breathless With Her

Book 2: Reckless With You

Book 3: Shameless With Him

Redwood Pack Series:

Book 1: An Alpha's Path

Book 2: A Taste for a Mate

Book 3: Trinity Bound

Book 3.5: A Night Away

Book 4: Enforcer's Redemption

Book 4.5: Blurred Expectations

Book 4.7: Forgiveness

Book 5: Shattered Emotions

Book 6: Hidden Destiny

Book 6.5: A Beta's Haven

Book 7: Fighting Fate

Book 7.5: Loving the Omega

Book 7.7: The Hunted Heart

Book 8: Wicked Wolf

The Talon Pack:

Book 1: Tattered Loyalties

Book 2: An Alpha's Choice

Book 3: Mated in Mist

Book 4: Wolf Betrayed

Book 5: Fractured Silence

Book 6: Destiny Disgraced

Book 7: Eternal Mourning

Book 8: Strength Enduring

Book 9: Forever Broken

The Elements of Five Series:

Book 1: From Breath and Ruin

Book 2: From Flame and Ash

Book 3: From Spirit and Binding

Book 4: From Shadow and Silence

The Branded Pack Series:
(Written with Alexandra Ivy)

Book 1: Stolen and Forgiven

Book 2: Abandoned and Unseen

Book 3: Buried and Shadowed

Dante's Circle Series:

Book 1: Dust of My Wings

Book 2: Her Warriors' Three Wishes

Book 3: An Unlucky Moon

Book 3.5: His Choice

Book 4: Tangled Innocence

Book 5: Fierce Enchantment

Book 6: An Immortal's Song

Book 7: Prowled Darkness

Book 8: Dante's Circle Reborn

Holiday, Montana Series:

Book 1: Charmed Spirits

Book 2: Santa's Executive

Book 3: Finding Abigail

Book 4: Her Lucky Love

Book 5: Dreams of Ivory

The Happy Ever After Series:

Flame and Ink

Ink Ever After

Single Title:

Finally Found You